AT NIGH
LIFTS WEIGHTS

Kang Young-sook

Translated from the Korean by
Janet Hong

**TRANSIT
BOOKS**

Published by Transit Books
1569 Solano Ave #142, Berkeley, CA 94707
www.transitbooks.org

© Kang Young-sook, 2011
Translation copyright © Janet Hong, 2023
All rights reserved by and controlled through Barbara J. Zitwer Agency
Originally published in Korean by Changbi Publishers, Inc.
in Korea in 2011

ISBN: 978-1-945492-70-9 (PAPERBACK)

LIBRARY OF CONGRESS CONTROL NUMBER: 2023941707

DESIGN & TYPESETTING
JUSTIN CARDER

PRINTED IN THE UNITED STATES OF AMERICA

9 8 7 6 5 4 3 2 1

*This book is published with the support of the Literature Translation Institute
of Korea (LTI Korea).*

Contents

From Mullae

THE CAR REEKED OF CHOCOLATE. The forty-year-old ate it every waking moment, turning all that he touched sweet and sticky. My job was to remove the chocolate traces he left behind with a wet wipe. I didn't mind. After all, he was my man.

From time to time, dreary buildings of an obscure purpose popped up on either side of the road. The forest bordering the road was mostly brown. I didn't want to leave the city. The scene we passed through reminded me of deserted buildings you'd see in a horror movie, LEGO structures with gaping sections, like toothless mouths. We entered District Y and continued on the country road for about ten minutes before we finally stopped. I recalled seeing a half-faded name near the top of an apartment building.

"Isn't that it? Did you see it?" he cried, as if to himself.

He put the car in reverse and turned off the engine. To our right, an apartment building called Bluebird something-or-other jutted from a field at an unnatural angle. He yanked up the hand brake, and I pulled out another wet wipe to erase the chocolate he'd smeared on it.

Three months ago, we had stopped around here and squinted through the car window, like settlers newly arrived on the frontier. The twelve-story building was erected on a bare field, which started barely a hundred meters from the road. There was no fence, not even a low wall, and no other facilities, like a children's playground slide. The frozen patches of snow, drilled into the ground like so many dots, and the swish of the whirling wind—these were the only things I registered. Behind the apartment several paddy fields stretched to the hills, and even the hills were all farmland. Frequent billboards displaying illustrations of cows let you know you'd entered an agricultural zone.

As soon as I opened the window, an acrid tang, difficult to describe, like the smell of rain hitting the scorched earth, surged into my throat. He twisted around in his seat, looking for his cigarettes. I followed him out of the car. While I narrowed my eyes and peered about me, the stench kept burrowing into my body. It smelled like baked dust, clammy metal, a polluted river.

He smoked, leaning against the driver's side window. I stepped off the sidewalk onto the field and walked toward the apartment. The winter sun was blinding. I stared up at the balconies that faced the road. White sheets flapped in the wind, and I heard a door open and shut, and someone's hacking cough. But no, I'd only imagined these things. I saw nothing and I heard nothing.

"Let's go wait in the car!" he cried, waving his hand.

I turned up my collar against the cold. Freight trucks barreled past, kicking up dust. I finally identified the oppressive smell that hung in the air. It was death. The same smell I'd detected in the middle of the room when I was young, that frightening smell I'd been forced to accept.

"This is the perfect place for you. You can have a fresh cup of milk every morning. You'll get better in no time. Happy? Why shouldn't you be?"

With a hand sheathed in a leather glove, he pointed at the billboard of cows on the side of the road and patted my shoulder. R wouldn't stop at milk. He'd bring me a whole cow, if he thought it'd be good for me. The ground beneath us started vibrating just then and a military truck as big as a tank came charging down the road. We got back in the car, shivering from the cold. The paddy fields behind the apartment had already grown dark. An hour had gone by, but there was still no sign of the real estate agent.

"Where the hell is he?"

Several times, R picked up his cell phone and flung it down.

"You sure he's coming?" I asked. "Did you talk to him? Maybe he forgot."

He dozed, arms crossed over his chest. Big snowflakes fell on the windshield. Without thinking, I leaned forward and opened my mouth. I must have been very thirsty. Right then two children sprung out from the east entrance of the apartment. Both were wearing long padded jackets and masks decorated with animal faces. Holding hands, they walked across the field and stepped onto the sidewalk. They glanced at us as they walked past. After a few steps, the smaller child looked back once more. I raised my hand in an awkward wave. Ignoring me, they quickly walked along the narrow road, still holding hands. Each time a truck hurtled past them, I couldn't help holding my breath.

• • •

Our last day in Mullae was exhausting. To be honest, I had zero expectations about District Y, where we were moving for my husband's work. We'd been comfortable in Mullae, a dim and dingy neighborhood, once home to many textile mills. When the mills added *Inc.* to their names and moved into office buildings, the alleys were overtaken by small-scale ironworks and the smell of machine grease. The snowbanks piled on street corners were always dirty and the last on earth to melt. All the dust in Seoul seemed to collect in Mullae.

I don't know at what point artists started to gather between Mullae station and Yeongdeungpo station, driven out from the pricier side of the Han River. While many metal fabrication and welding shops still remained, vacant workshops received new coats of paint and were converted into art studios. Flowers emblazoned on a shop door. Characters in a mural. For some strange reason, these splashes of color suited the gray neighborhood. Early in the morning, it was the industrial workers who strode along the alleys. Not that the artists came out at night. Most of the time they stayed in their studios. Sometimes, though, they came out for a late-night drink, and could be seen sitting at a table next to the ironworkers.

Boksun's Place was where these two unlikely groups came together. With a large sunflower painted on its sign, it was the only nice restaurant in Mullae. The ironworkers weren't a talkative bunch. For the first hour, all they did was consume the liquor and meat before them, heads tilted toward the table at similar angles. They ate and drank until their foreheads shone with grease, oblivious to the fact their mouths were ringed with soot. At last, when they'd filled their bellies, they began to talk about their day. Though they tended to be crude and vulgar, they never bothered anybody else.

At the next table, artists with long hair and bright clothes ate and smoked and drank soju. They were just as quiet as the ironworkers, but possessed a lively energy. After sitting in such proximity to the young artists, I loved walking out at the end of the night and seeing the gray sky flushing red in the distance. With hardly any streetlights, the streets grew dark around seven o'clock, but still I shivered from happiness.

There was a girl. She went in and out of the restaurant kitchen, helping the owner trim soybean sprouts and fetching beer and soju from the cooler for the customers sometimes. She smoked freely with the factory men nearly double her age, not thinking twice about borrowing their lighters. But whenever anyone said or did something she didn't like, she flew into a rage and screamed, "I'm an artist, goddamn it, a frigging painter!" Then the other artists filled their shot glasses with soju and drank to her, crying, "Yes, you're the best, bravo!" The ironworkers, however, cast their gazes to the floor with sheepish smiles, or tipped back their shot glasses with no change in their expressions.

I would come across her suddenly around the neighborhood. There she would be at Boksun's Place, at the public bath, in front of the produce truck, or on Rodeo Street—there was always a Rodeo Street or a Rodeo Karaoke in every lousy city I'd ever lived in. Her hair was styled differently each time: in pigtails that hung down past her collarbone, or twisted up in a topknot, or strewn loose across her shoulders. Still, I recognized her instantly. She possessed an unusual, restless energy and never stopped moving, not even for a second. I'd thought I would run into her at least once more before we moved to District Y, but I didn't.

The first time I ever saw her was at a supermarket checkout. Before the clerk had finished tallying up her bill, she'd wandered over to another aisle to browse through other items. "Excuse me, Ms. XXX, could you sign here please?"

I couldn't help but smile. We had the exact same name. How could such a pretty girl have the same name as me and also live in Mullae? I clasped my hands together in sheer delight. It made me want to stop everyone in the street and shake their hand.

She signed the card reader and smoothed down her frizzy hair. After hollering a "thank you," she clomped out of the store in ankle boots and purple pants. I followed her. With a plastic bag in hand, she headed to Boksun's Place. Seated between other young artists, she looked five, no, ten years younger than me. Soon afterwards, my husband and his colleagues came into the restaurant as if we'd arranged to meet there. One of the artists unwrapped a muffler from around his neck and put it around the girl's shoulders. She and her friends kept snickering, while eating kimchi stew and drinking soju. Then she glanced at me.

I didn't want to miss the moment, but I quickly turned away. A short while later, I looked at her out of the corner of my eye. Maybe I'd only imagined it, but I was sure she'd been looking at me, too. She was beautiful, but odd, constantly placing kisses on her friends' noses. For some reason, my belly grew warm whenever I watched her. An artist with my name, and a painter at that!

On our last evening in Mullae, I joined my husband and his co-workers for dinner at Boksun's Place. As always, we ambled home after, one by one wending their way to the bus stop or alley, until the only ones left were me, my husband, and an older bachelor, of whom my husband was especially fond. He was a large man. He kept throwing his arms around my husband in a bear hug.

"Ah, come on now," my husband kept saying, as he hugged the older man's head to his chest and placed a kiss on top. He slung his arm around the man's shoulders.

Such strange men. I stood off to the side like a streetlight, watching the clumsy affection between the two lumbering men, and followed at a distance when they started off again.

Soon we arrived at the man's house. They embraced each other once more. Just then, noise flooded into the dark alley and the young artists passed by. I saw a flash of purple. It was the girl! But the group vanished.

After some time, I slipped my arm through my husband's, and he put his arm around my shoulders. Though we were in a dangerous part of town, I wasn't afraid when he was with me.

As soon as we opened the gate to our multi-unit, the sensor light on the first floor came on, shutting off when the light on the second floor switched on. I gazed down at the alley until everything went dark again. I looked and looked, but saw no one. After I'd helped my husband lie down and pulled off his socks for him, I headed back out. I'd never walked the alley alone at night, but I wasn't scared.

I rushed out onto the main street and crossed the road, as if I had some urgent business, heading for the five-way intersection where the artists' studios were located. I seemed to have lost my mind. The streets were slippery, but I was in a hurry. The ironworks nearby had closed hours earlier. The men sometimes put up plastic sheets and worked well into the night, but most of the industrial shops were shuttered and their interiors pitch black. I strode down an alley and stopped at a studio that still had its light on, nestled in between the dark workshops. I stood on tiptoe and peered into the tinted window. I saw the girl. I had found her.

The back of her head looked small and her hands extremely big. The table was cluttered with every kind of liquor bottle, from wine to soju to beer, and her enormous canvas was unspeakably dark. Behind the easel, paintings lined the wall, but I didn't have a clue what they were about. A headless, legless torso from which a giant eye stared out. A figure floating in the air, the head detached from the body. There was one painting that was completely black. The girl sat in a corner, staring blankly at the canvases or down at her phone.

My God, I found myself trying to go inside! Luckily, the door was locked. Even though her paintings were so frightening, I didn't have a nightmare that night. I'd never told anyone how I used to get down on my knees every night to pray I wouldn't have a bad dream. That's the kind of fool I was. But whenever I thought about the girl, I grew calm and meek, like a tamed animal.

• • •

The real estate agent knocked on the car window with a leather-gloved hand. Only then did I see his old Sonata parked behind us.

"Everyone dreams of this country life," he said as he removed his knit cap. He seemed to smirk, pointing at the billboard where cows flashed massive udders and human smiles. "Now you can have a fresh cup of milk every morning."

It was a line I'd heard many times. I kept my sunglasses on, half-listening. I wasn't ready to accept the fact that we were a long way from Mullae.

As soon as we entered the suite, the agent fished out a bundle of newspaper from his plastic bag and started to fan out the pages across the floor until the entire space was covered. The apartment got a lot of light and had a comfortable feel, apart from the noise of the traffic outside. The agent said the place would look cozy once the furniture came in.

As he circled the living room, he said all the typical things that estate agents say.

I opened the kitchen window that looked out onto the paddy fields in the back. I liked the way they stretched all the way to the hills.

"We'll take it."

The estate agent gave a wide smile and awkwardly opened his arms. "Why don't we head to the office then?"

My husband stepped out of the bathroom and said with a laugh that he'd do as I wished. The estate agent walked toward the front door. I followed him to the entrance and turned, gazing at the newspaper laid out on the floor. The agent had left red footprints wherever he'd stepped. It was blood.

But with nowhere else to go, we had no choice but to move in.

The shouts of children woke me in the morning. I opened the front door, but the hallway was quiet. Sunlight streamed in through the windows. It was too cold to open the large living-room window, so I opened the small window above the kitchen sink. Children stood in a circle, staring at the ground. Black objects big and small dotted the frozen paddy fields.

"They're dead!" the children shouted. "The birds are all dead!"

I squeezed my eyes shut. Dead birds littered the white fields. I put on a sweater and slid open the big window. The cold wind rushed in. There was a black feather stuck in the frame. The second I stretched out my hand, the feather blew in and stuck to my chest.

Why had so many birds died here? It was difficult for someone like me to understand. Honestly, I didn't know a thing. I couldn't even begin to guess the cause. All day I watched the news and ate peanuts. District Y wasn't the only place to experience mass bird deaths. There were reports of mass bird deaths all over the country. The cause was unclear. Experts speculated that trauma, bad weather, or the noise from local fireworks were to blame. I had to tell my husband about the dead birds, there was so much to tell him, but he didn't come home.

He returned close to midnight. He looked noticeably thinner. I clasped his face in my hands, but he didn't crack a smile. He'd always brought back news from the outside world. I believed everything he said. After all, I was frail and he was strong. I knew nothing and he knew everything. I lay down with my head in his lap.

"There was blood in the valley stream," he said. "It was all frozen and snow was falling on top."

The smell of blood bothered me. I pushed my head between his legs. I put my nose to his jacket and sniffed the fishy, copper stink. He stroked my face and hair with his broad hand.

"I have to head out early in the morning. I just want to go to bed."

He looked exhausted. He cried out several times in his sleep.

• • •

I heard the hair dryer, and the cabinet door open and close.

"Don't go outside. It's supposed to be freezing today," my husband said to me while I was still half asleep. Soon after, I heard the front door close.

Cold mornings are unbearable for people with low blood pressure. I could barely lift my head and place my feet on the floor. Luckily, I didn't collapse back onto the bed. I opened the curtains and window, and smelled the wind blowing in from the paddy fields. The news was going on about the mass bird deaths again. Several hundreds of dead birds had fallen from the sky in downtown Hong Kong, and about five hundred had died in a small Japanese village due to a sudden cold spell. All over the world thousands of birds had been found dead, in the southern part of the United States, Finland, and Sweden.

Every morning the milkman placed a glass bottle of fresh organic milk outside our door, but there were no deliveries that day. I discovered a thick feather in the frame of the small corridor window, which looked out onto the back paddies. I took it inside and stuck it in the empty milk bottle where I had placed the feather from the other day.

My husband was still not home past midnight. I finally fell asleep. When I woke in the middle of the night and climbed out of bed, I discovered him in the living room. He was sitting on the floor drinking soju, illuminated by just a small lamp. My husband—a large man—looked strangely small. I sat behind him and started massaging his shoulders. His shoulders were tense.

"Did you wash up?"

He shook his head.

"Did you run into an old lover then?"

He shook his head once more.

"Isn't it dark? Should I turn on the room light?" I said, pretending to be cheerful. "You really need to wash. You smell bad."

He got to his feet and went to the bathroom. I caught another whiff of the stench from where he'd been sitting.

I went into the bathroom after he came out. The floor by the bathtub looked a bit red. I brushed a finger along the tiles. A film of oil came off on my finger. Strands of his hair were caught in the sink, but the stench overpowered everything. I broke out in goosebumps again.

In bed I stroked his back. He was still awake.

"Can you hold me for a bit?" I asked.

He turned and put his arms around me. He still smelled of blood.

"Promise me you won't go outside," he said, as if I were a child. He held me tightly, tucking my head under his chin. "It freaks me out to be a human walking around on two legs."

All night I slipped in and out of nightmares. It was hard to bear the noise from the suite upstairs. Anyone would have assumed an important soccer match was on. The toilet flushed, a woman screamed, a man swore. I lay with the blanket pulled over my face, clutching the edge of the fabric. When the fight upstairs finally ended, I heard snoring. The woman kept crying. In the end, I must have fallen asleep, because her crying seeped into my dreams. I tore open the ceiling and climbed up. Light shone through the crack in the bathroom door. When I pushed the door open, I saw the woman hunched over on the toilet, weeping. I stroked her hair and begged, "Please, can you stop crying? My bed is right below and I can't sleep."

When she raised her face at last, it was the girl from Mullae. All strength left my legs, and I sank to the bathroom floor.

I kept wandering in and out of the girl's paintings. When I was gazing at a painting of a horse's severed head, my foot fell in and then my arm, until my face was touching the severed head. But there was no blood, and the horse didn't make a sound. Did this mean something had happened to the girl? I hoped she was okay.

In the morning, I braced myself and stepped outside. The sun shone brightly, but the wind was fierce. There were three tents set up in the vacant lot across the apartment. They hadn't been there a few days earlier. I crossed the street to have a look. A woman in black stood in front of the tents, holding a bundle of pamphlets.

"Ma'am, you've got to read this! Don't just stand there, come and have a look. This district has become a place of death. You need to get out of here. Just forget everything and go!"

She tried to come closer. I was scared of her dark eyebrows. I dodged the speeding cars and managed to make it back across. By the apartment entrance, young children were poking a dead bird with sticks, and middle-school boys were standing around smoking. The pamphlets that had blown in from the tents flapped madly as they sailed toward the field.

I strode around the building and headed for the fields. Unable to stop, I stumbled right into the paddies. I stared at the farms in the distance, but didn't think I could make it there in my condition. Still, I set out blindly. I needed to know what was happening. My feet sank into the mud that hadn't frozen over. I looked back at the apartment that grew smaller and smaller like a scale model each time I passed over a ridge. When I got closer to the hills, I heard a different noise. I was scared. If I crossed one more ridge, I would be at the brow, which was the entrance point to the farms. Right then, trucks started to file out of the agricultural zone onto the unpaved road. The air was thick with the stench of pigs. Terrified, I pressed the speed dial on my phone without thinking. My husband didn't pick up.

The soles of my shoes were filthy. Before I went back into the apartment building, I found an outdoor tap in the back beside the dumpsters. Luckily it wasn't frozen. As soon as I twisted the tap, icy water gushed out. The water that washed off my shoes onto the patch of cement was red. I dropped the rubber hose and raced toward the entrance. The kids who had been smoking were still there. I stood next to them, panting.

"Let's go kill a dog, too," they said, flicking away their cigarette butts.

My husband returned around midnight with two bottles of soju.

"Why not just buy them by the box?" I said. I stroked his cheek. "You've been drinking every night since we moved here."

He let out a heavy sigh and started to say something.

"No. Don't tell me what's happening out there."

As if he understood, he stretched out his legs and laid me down on the floor next to him. "I can't remember the last time I held my wife. How about we do a little something tonight?"

The dark living room lit up whenever a car passed by, shining its headlights into the window, and falling dark once more. I twisted around and gazed at his face. Unbuttoning his pants with one hand, I brought my mouth between his legs. There was the smell of blood again. I pushed up his shirt with one hand and fumbled for his penis. I couldn't find it. The window lit up and grew dark, repeatedly, at greater and greater intervals.

"Don't tell me anything," I said, looking up at his face. "I don't want to know."

• • •

The next morning, there was a knock at the door. I answered it after the doorbell had rung several times. Smiling women were gripping pamphlets, their faces raw and red from the cold. They had come from an animal protection group. I found it difficult to listen to what they had to say and gazed toward the window the entire time. I kept licking the roof of my mouth. It felt as if something was starting to bud on the tip of my tongue.

I hardly budged all day. I sat in the same spot on the living room floor, and took down and put back the objects that were within arm's reach. I even flipped through our wedding album. When I'd first told my friends that I was getting married, they had opened their eyes wide and waved their hands in front of their faces.

"Don't do it! He's going to eat you up!" one had said. "How can you marry someone with a face like that?"

Still I tried to convince them that he was a good and caring man, and not some barbaric animal as they thought, but they didn't believe me. He really was a good, caring man.

Then for some reason, after we were married, my body started to break down.

My husband's relatives, who'd always told me they liked me because I was so strong and robust, now asked what was the matter each time we met. My husband had expected to fill the house with a brood of boys who took after him. He'd believed they would be his ticket to retirement. I sensed his disappointment, even though he never voiced anything of that sort.

Strictly speaking, it wasn't my fault. Plus, I liked the fact it was just us two. There were too many cars, the Arctic glaciers were melting at an alarming rate, buildings were constantly collapsing, wars were breaking out everywhere, and the world was full of cancer patients. The last thing I wanted to do was leave behind children in this world. I had no desire to keep even a dog or cat as a pet. My resolve never wavered. After all, I had my husband to keep me company.

I heard the key in the door. My husband staggered in looking sloppy and bedraggled, as if he'd been in a steam room until now. His entire body was wet. He sank to his knees and hunched over on the floor.

"That bad?" I could hardly talk because of the canker sore.

He stayed frozen in that position, his cheek stuck to the living room floor. I removed his shoes and socks. His insoles were wet. The hairs on my arms stood up, and my face stung as if the skin had grown too tight. My taste buds seemed to swell more and more until they filled my mouth.

He didn't want to eat. He couldn't because of the nausea. He crawled to the bed, and I filled a small plastic basin with water, and washed his face and hands. All evening he burned with a high fever. He kept moaning and would suddenly sit up as if to vomit, and then lie back down again. Many times, I wet a towel with cold water and placed it on his head. I nearly forgot about my canker sore.

He woke in the middle of the night. I found him in his thermals in the living room, eating a chocolate bar. He looked fine, but something in his expression made him appear strange and rather simple. We sat side by side with our shoulders touching and ate chocolate non-stop. We ate until the smell of chocolate overpowered everything and our heads went numb.

There was a commotion across the street. The women in black were by the tents again. Things turned clamorous whenever they appeared. They'd been there since morning, holding signs that screamed: *The world ended in the 60s!*

So the world had ended before I was even born. In District Y alone, two thousand pigs had been slaughtered. It was a number I couldn't fathom.

"Shame on you, wicked officials, for slaughtering pigs without compensating farmers!"

I shook my head. I didn't want to listen to the voice on the speakers.

The middle-school boys who had huddled by the apartment entrance now smoked across the street by the tents. Right then I saw a procession of trucks come out from the farms. There were over ten of them. Covered with black tarp, they sped down the dirt lane, leaving behind a strange odor. I wanted to know what would heal my tongue. It felt as if it was going to start bleeding, but I had no choice but to put up with it. The canker sore, the smell, the voice coming through the speakers—they were all too much to bear.

The next day, my husband had to leave early for work.

"Don't go outside," he said, as if making a vow.

In the afternoon, I got into our old car and sped along the road where the trucks with the pigs had gone. Government agents in masks and white plastic suits stood at the entrance point of the hills, controlling access to the area. Regular traffic was not permitted to enter. They told me to turn back immediately. I couldn't hear what they said. All they did was wave their batons in the air. My tongue hurt, and I was terrified.

"I'm supposed to meet my husband," I said. "He works here. He asked me to bring him something."

But they just shook their heads at me. I saw the sun starting to fall behind the hills.

"I'll stop here then. I won't go in. I'll wait for him here, I promise!"

I parked the car on the side of the road and sat inside for a long time. About an hour later, when their shift ended, the agents got in a car and drove off.

There was a valley to my left. I walked up the steep dirt lane marked by numerous tire tracks. I hadn't climbed very far when the hill leveled out abruptly and I saw a strange sight. It was a giant pit, with an enormous mound swelling up from it, a mound endlessly vast and wide, like a vessel from outer space. Empty trucks surrounded the bulge, and people in masks and white plastic suits were pulling a massive canvas sheet over it—no, it was closer to a white foil tarp. They grabbed the edge of the tarp and dragged it to the center, continuing to the opposite rim. Trucks rumbled past constantly, and I heard shrill whistles and the crackling of walkie-talkie radios. I didn't see my husband. A little while later, everything grew chaotic as they marched in and out of the pit to tamp down the tarp. I pictured all the pig carcasses inside. The vast pile of carcasses rotting and disintegrating inside the pit.

The sun was setting unbelievably fast. I couldn't find my husband. Steam rose from the white mound. Agents in plastic suits kept tugging the tarp over the bulge. Nausea welled up in me. I wondered if this is what morning sickness felt like. *See? What a pain*, I mumbled. *Thank God I'm not pregnant.*

I needed to go home. I glanced around me before heading down to the car. The hills were growing dark at an alarming rate, and the lights down by the road were starting to come on one by one. The pit was darkening, too. I was about to make my way down the hill when I glanced back. Then in that unhappy moment I saw her—the girl from Mullae.

In purple pants, with her long hair streaming behind her, she dashed over the white mound of entangled carcasses. She swung her arms like an action painter, like a small insect dancing. All I could do was stand rooted in the same spot and watch. Darkness fell over District Y. When I could no longer see the pit or the girl, I stumbled down the hill.

I turned on the engine and started to drive. The car was almost out of gas. There was nowhere left to go. I went slowly along the dirt lane. Up ahead, I saw a disinfection checkpoint. When had they set it up? The cars in front of me slowed to a stop. A lighted sign warned that all vehicles exiting infected premises must undergo decontamination.

I hoped the fumes of slaughter rising from the pit would not reach Mullae. I hoped the blood seeping into the soil from the pit would not reach the girl.

The car ahead was finished. It was my turn. All of a sudden, I missed my husband. I wanted to tell him that now—now was the time for us to love each other. I kept looking back to see if his car was coming. At that very moment, sprayers began to blast my car with disinfectant.

At Night He Lifts Weights

MY SISTER—now dead—wiped the wetness from her eyes. You have to die before I do, she said. How else will you survive on your own? I should look after you forever.

Though elderly herself, she worried about me, because I was the youngest. Around sunset, we sisters walked into the market as dark as a coffin. We liked to recite the names of seasonal greens and fruits while watching scuffles break out. A black plastic bag containing things like pickled vegetables and salted mackerel usually dangled from my sister's hand. This supply was enough to last us for a few days.

We didn't go home right away. We stopped by an electronics store and checked out the newest model of kimchi refrigerators. We sat inside an ice cream shop packed with high school students in uniform and ate ice cream, wincing all the while from the pain of sensitive teeth. We laughed over funny stories, occasionally wetting ourselves.

"You too? Me too!"

We cackled when we realized we'd both pissed our pants. If children were playing on the street, we squatted and played with them for a long time. After a dinner of red bean soup or knife noodles with clams, we finally headed home.

Such indulgences came to an end once my sister's illness grew worse. She didn't dare go outside unless the day was warm, without a single breath of wind.

If she wanted to say something, she practically sprang up, limbs bouncing off the wheelchair, like a dry branch snapping in a fire. Then splayed out across the seat, she would start to bring up the gruel or barely tea I had spooned into her mouth just moments before. A shocking amount of liquid gushed out of her eyes, her nose, her mouth. Whenever this happened, I couldn't help but grow angry. The time I'd spent feeding her seemed a complete waste. Her body kept drying up.

Was it just a phase? Right before she died, moisture oozed endlessly from her parched body. All at once, she withered, looking like a naked branch from a persimmon tree. Then, like the puffy clouds that hung in the sky but disappeared as night approached, my sister left this world.

My eyes grew dimmer after she died. I needed reading glasses to read the newspaper. When I closed my eyes, the face of my mother, long dead, overlapped with the faces of my dead sisters, and together, they rose before me. I needed to put my thoughts in order.

On the left, I drew a circle for my father whose face I could no longer recall, and on the right, I drew a circle for my mother. I added a vertical line below and six circles below that, writing the names of my siblings inside the circles and then marking all those who had died with an X. Every time one of them had left me, I'd become smaller, more alone. Everything before my eyes had become hollow, like puddles dried to monstrous shapes. Still, it was exhilarating there was no one left to nag me, no matter what I did. But one thing became clear after my sister's death: It was my turn next.

It's been three days since the toilet broke down. I raised the lid and sat on the floor outside the bathroom with the door open, observing the broken toilet. I'd been calling the neighborhood repair shop for the past two days, but the plumber didn't come. I described the situation in detail to whoever answered the phone, as if I were explaining the symptoms of a sick puppy to a veterinarian. The more I stared at the toilet, the more I grew worried that the contents inside would spew out.

. . .

Splash.

It was finally overflowing! I squeezed my eyes shut, picturing the disgusting sight. A dark, gleaming object flew out of the toilet bowl. It was a bird. It flitted out of the small bathroom and hit the living room fluorescent light before escaping through the balcony door. It took all but three seconds for it to appear and then disappear. The blink of an eye.

I needed to take a leak. I pulled out a red plastic pail with a lid from the balcony storage room. After tugging down my pants, I squatted over the pail. I closed the lid and placed it beside the toilet. I needed to eat less, at least while I used the pail.

I climbed onto the toilet and opened the small window above. The autumn blue sky flooded in. I couldn't help thrusting my face toward it. I heard a siren. There had been another accident at the rubber factory. The men there kept dying from some inexplicable cause. While the cause of death was being investigated, the factory continued to pump out tires and floor mats. The siren became jumbled with other noises: the loudspeakers from the produce trucks, the yelping of the puppy from the apartment downstairs, the cries of children in the playground. I sensed someone come to my door. As soon as I opened it, a flyer that had been wedged in the door dropped to the ground.

• • •

A few months ago, a fifteen-year-old girl in a plaid school uniform was found dead on the beach near the industrial complex. Her body was left on the sands contaminated by red tide, in a conspicuous spot under some branches, as if the killer had wanted the crime to be discovered. There were severe injuries and a stab wound to the genital area, as well as evidence of sexual assault. Her schoolbag, propped against her hip, was stuffed to bursting. Individually wrapped jumbo fish sausages that had been swaddled in the girl's underwear spilled out. In this area, sausages were no longer snacks but instruments of rape and murder. Rumors of sausage manufacturers going out of business began to spread.

Before a single clue surfaced about the killer, another incident took place last night. In the residential area west of the industrial complex, a woman was found murdered in her basement flat. There were no signs of rape, and she was lying on her side with her hands tied behind her back. The front door was closed without any indication of forced entry, and even the window with its iron grates that looked out onto the street was locked as usual. After returning from cram school, her son had rung the doorbell repeatedly. He'd then called her cell phone many times, but she hadn't picked up. That's when he'd called the police. Spread out across the living room table were kimchi and salted seafood, along with grains of rice, as if someone with a voracious appetite had eaten. However, the autopsy revealed the woman's stomach was empty. She had no family other than her son. The whole town was terrified and couldn't sleep.

Women stood talking noisily in front of the maintenance office. They pulled out their cell phones and called their daughters at school and their younger sisters at work, warning them to be careful.

"Our rotten educational system is to blame!"

"What does the educational system have anything to do with it?" a woman said, carrying a bag of food scraps. "It's because this neighborhood is lousy!"

She disappeared in the direction of the garbage room.

Every night, the wind blew in from the direction of the industrial complex. I didn't mind. My older sister used to say the reason she'd die earlier than others her age was because of pollution. She claimed it was my fault for moving into an apartment near an industrial complex. But I didn't feel the same way. I liked watching the white smoke billow up from the smokestacks in the middle of the night. Whenever I saw that sight, I couldn't help thinking that the world was operating as it should. If she wanted to live in a better neighborhood, away from factories, she should have pitched in. But she hadn't contributed anything.

At the corner of the flower bed outside my building, I opened the lid of my red pail. Bravely, I poured the contents into the flower bed where chrysanthemums and hibiscus bloomed. Relief flooded me. The pail made a pinging sound each time it bumped against my knee.

As I was passing the playground, I came to a stop. There was a man under the streetlight. Shirtless, he curled and uncurled a dumbbell. It wasn't cold, but I shivered. Slowly I walked around the playground. I walked as slowly as possible, because I wanted to see his face, but he didn't turn around.

The plumber came when I was watching the evening news. After raising the toilet cover, he stuck a long thin metal rod into the bowl and peered inside. He continued to peer inside, even after the news had covered politics, top stories, and global affairs. He turned on a small fan heater and warmed up the inside of the toilet. At last, he inserted a metal hose and poured a harsh-smelling chemical into it. I got to my feet, wondering when he would ever finish, but he came out of the bathroom just then.

"It's unclogged now."

With his bag squeezed under his arm, he shoved his gloves into the pocket of his navy-blue jacket and gave a polite bow.

"Thank you. Can I give you a cup of coffee before you go?"

He'd been putting his shoes on in a hurry, but he stopped and scanned the apartment. "Granny, you've got to be care-ful. Don't invite any old salesman inside, all right? Even if you're lonely."

What insolence! He seemed a completely different per-son from the polite young man who'd just bowed to me. The second he left, shutting the door with a bang, I ran to the bathroom and sat on the toilet. The piss I'd been holding for a long time gushed out.

With the flyer in hand, I headed to the side street lined with eateries and cram schools. Bored of staying home all day long, I decided to get a part-time job at the gimbap shop. I figured rolling gimbap would be easy, but it was harder than I thought. Students came and went, wearing out the doorsill. After eating gimbap, spicy rice cakes, and fish cakes, which they paid for by putting their change together, boys and girls huddled in the narrow street and spewed cigarette smoke.

Soon my starched green apron became splattered and soggy with grease. Thirty thousand won for four hours of work—it didn't seem bad. They said you could make more than sixty thousand won a day as a housecleaner. That would have been better, of course, but I didn't have the courage to barge into a stranger's house and wash their dishes and put them away and iron their clothes and hang them up in the closet.

The grilled rice shop across the street was also packed with customers. They were the busiest at lunch, but even after the lunchtime rush, an endless stream of customers went into the shop. A man wearing a black-and-white checkered shirt sat scrubbing a grill pan very slowly behind the shop window that looked out onto the street. My eyes were drawn to his muscular forearms that showed below his rolled-up sleeves. I quickly got my bag from the locker, put on my glasses, and stared at him through the window. His brawny body didn't match his lined face. He was old, close to my age.

At eight in the evening, after work, I persuaded a co-worker to go eat at the grilled rice shop with me. The old man in the checkered shirt came toward us, holding a black grill.

"So what can I get you ladies?"

I almost laughed out loud at his tacky line. His dark forearms gleamed, a stark contrast against his white gloves, and his gray hair and lean, angular face were at odds with his physique. He was very busy. He put in our order, went back to his spot by the window to scrub the grill, answered the phone, and waited on tables. While the cabbage and mushroom cooked on our pan, he headed outside.

"Do you know him?"

I looked away from him and saw that my co-worker was peering at me. He was smoking, sitting in a chair right outside the door. Judging from the way his head was tilted, I tried to guess what he was staring at. The slim legs of the girls passing by? Or the faces of the men from the factories? I couldn't tell.

"You want to come to church with me this weekend?"

She was a devout believer and I was the target of her evangelism. The man's shoulders appeared extremely broad. I was sure he was the same man from the playground who'd been lifting weights.

I bought myself a track suit, a white one with a hood and green stripe running down the side of the pants. I planned to take a walk on Tuesdays, Thursdays, and on the weekends in the afternoon when I didn't have to work. Those who don't exercise are lazy, whether they're old or young, and I hated to become one of them.

I set out blindly along the highway near Complex 1, which was the site of many car accidents. A truck driver slowed down to tell me to wear a mask. A bundle of books that had fallen off a moving truck bounced along the road.

If I grew tired, I went into the neighborhood church. People from different Asian counties drank tea and talked in the church courtyard. A person talked on the phone inside a telephone booth for a long time. Flyers the police had distributed concerning the horrific murders littered the ground.

On some days, I walked too much. I would look up and find myself very far from home. Unseasonable cold winds blew. The factories, which had always loomed before me, were now in the distant west. I tried to stop, but couldn't. I was approaching the trail around the reclaimed lake near the industrial complex. The lake had been decaying for decades. The trail stretched on in silence.

On that slightly winding trail, I glimpsed a checkered shirt for a second before I lost sight of it. Too preoccupied with humming, I couldn't trust my eyes. Right then a tall girl with long hair came into view. She was walking beside a man in a checkered shirt. With her left hand placed awkwardly on the hand he offered her, he led her to the back of the lake. The trail flattened out as it curved around the lake, and I could taste the rotten stench at the back of my throat.

I flinched as a flock of birds surged up through the trees. When the temperature dipped, I wondered if I should have bought a thicker training suit. The sky was darkening and I could no longer see his checkered shirt. Had I seen correctly? I stood on my toes and scanned my surroundings. For a long time, I stood in the same spot, but didn't see a single person out for a stroll or a dog that had lost its way, so I started heading back.

I had a dream that night. It was the first time my sister appeared to me. We were swimming in deep waters toward a lush green valley. Right then, a large seal darted between us and leapt out of the water. We put our arms around it and rode it like a horse; we played and swam freely, like the seal that tried to swim away. My sister's body seemed smooth and firm, but the face I confronted above the surface was black and blue, like that of a corpse.

Two days later, the news reported the rape and murder of a high school girl whose body had been found in a lake next to the trail. It was the same decaying lake. I sprang to my feet in shock. The local news station's camera panned the trail and zoomed in on the lake. I'd been on the trail only two days earlier. Upon seeing the bloated corpse, the police concluded the girl had slipped and fallen into the lake or committed suicide. But soon after they moved the body, indications of rape and murder that had been concealed by the bloating were exposed. Her nipples had been lacerated and her genital area was mutilated. Everyone set out to find a witness. The girl's mother fainted and sat bolt upright, while the girl's uncle vowed to find and kill the culprit himself.

It's the old man. He's the culprit.

He was lifting weights on the apartment playground, his shirt tossed onto the platform of the gazebo. I was panting heavily, but I couldn't turn a blind eye to something like this. After all, I was a responsible citizen. I needed to make sure it had been him and the girl I'd seen on the trail that day, but I grew frightened as soon as I saw his brawny silhouette. Plus, I had no idea what I was supposed to say to him, or what I was going to do once I'd made sure it was him. I stood trembling in the same spot, so terrified I couldn't move. But he approached me instead and grabbed my arm. He then flexed, causing his deltoid muscle to contract. When I saw his dark muscles rippling, I couldn't help but squeeze my eyes shut. In that instant, his large hand squeezed my hand. He was trying to take me somewhere. But when I opened my eyes again, he was back in his spot, doing bicep curls.

• • •

A foul, inexplicable smell enveloped the city. The stench of noxious grease spread to the residential area across from the industrial complex. At first, people reported a stale odor, which grew more serious, causing headaches. Both young and old suffering from swollen eyes and sore throats packed the neighborhood ophthalmologists' and ENT clinics to overflowing. To prevent the spread of infection, officials were sent to the city to investigate and sewers were disinfected twice a day. All traffic entering the city was subject to inspection. The footage from the surveillance cameras outside the tunnel entrance was analyzed to see if any vehicle entering the industrial complex was disposing hazardous waste in the middle of the night. The investigations, however, did nothing to help solve the stench. They only revealed incidental facts—so many relieved themselves on the road and so many groped each other in the privacy of their cars, completely unaware that they were being recorded. People complained that their already cheap real estate now meant squat and called for the immediate resignation of the mayor.

Every night I made gimbap. If I grew tired of the usual pickled radish, ham, and spinach, I used ingredients like asparagus, clams, and soybean paste. On some days, I steamed rice using brewed green tea and tried putting those steeped green tea leaves into the gimbap. After making rice and roasting seaweed for a while, my small apartment would become awash with steam and the smell of sesame oil, and I would grow dazed. As soon as I opened the window, a metallic stench surged in from the direction of the factories. If I grew exhausted and fell asleep, I startled awake to find a jumble of gimbap ingredients lying askew on the table, like lost children. Bloated to the point of bursting, the gimbap looked like a pile of coal.

Protests were held all over the city. Even the kids who had huddled outside the bathrooms, smoking until their faces turned yellow, came out onto the street to join the protest. Through the front window of the gimbap shop, I saw teenagers holding signs. They walked by, carrying dummies of the girls who had been raped and murdered.

"Find the culprit! Or we'll set this city on fire!" chanted a few anxious-looking kids in the front, but the kids behind them chattered and horsed around as if they were on a field trip.

An official statement was issued, saying the smell was due to a critical problem in the city's sewage system. The mothers of young children were the first to condemn the municipality. They raised their voices, demanding clean water to make their babies' formula. A bottled water company left cheap, low-quality bottles of water containing moderate amounts of toxins at every door, free of charge. Still, people fought over them.

It rained. The rain-soaked leaves fell at the same time and littered the street. Some people burned the leaves, but this did nothing to erase the stench from the city. Perhaps because the seasons had changed, but people seemed to have forgotten about the recent murders, and students stopped their protests. I continued to make gimbap day after day. And like someone performing a penance, I ate the gimbap for breakfast, lunch, and dinner. I finally realized what I was waiting for. Yet, no matter how long I waited, he didn't come. He didn't come to the playground and he didn't come to the grilled rice shop.

Once the rain stopped, the city became gloomy. Due to frequent disinfection, the sewer grates downtown turned gray with corrosion. When the sewers were scoured, the rats came out into the streets and froze to death, unable to withstand the cold. The cause of the stench wasn't discovered. I wandered the city, looking for him. Each time I saw a silhouette like his or someone in similar clothes, my heart sped up. But it wasn't easy to find him.

"Ah, this horrible smell."

At my words, he dropped from my ceiling to the ground, landing gracefully in a crouch. "I'll take care of that for you."

His mouth spewed a stream of white insulation tape. He pressed the tape along the window pane, creating a tight seal. The perspiration trickling down his body was as clear as glass. In his spandex T-shirt that showed off his forearms, he looked like a young man from the back. The instant I raised a finger to touch a bead of his sweat, he curled up and vanished into the ceiling.

I never ran into him outside my apartment. I stopped going out for walks and even stopped going to my part-time job at the gimbap shop, which I'd been considering quitting anyway, and stayed cooped up at home. He came any time during the day, whenever I called. He tightened my loose bedroom door hinges with a hammer. If I needed water, he brought me a large jar full of clean water. He removed the tattered tape from the door threshold and replaced it with a new one, so I no longer had the problem of my stockings catching on the old tape.

When he finished these jobs, I made him a meal. He polished off his bowl and had another, and like a child, he wasn't very good with chopsticks. Kimchi juice splattered the table, even the front of my shirt. When he finished eating, he went out onto the balcony and had a cigarette. He then read every page of the newspaper he'd brought. I'd doze off watching him, and when I would wake, he would be gone.

"Looks like you need a new television."

Had I complained that mine has no sound? One day, he came into the apartment, carrying a big TV on his shoulders. A flat-screen TV now sat where my staticky box television used to sit. As soon as he connected the cables and turned the power on, a brand-new world showed up on screen. Out of pride, I insisted on paying for the TV, but he sat watching the screen without a word and finally said, "I just happened to find what people threw out."

Then he disappeared.

Strange rumors started to circulate around town. They said the one responsible for the killings wasn't a notorious murderer or a felon with a long criminal record. Neither was it one of the girls' lover or boyfriend. Then who? They said the crimes were the work of the elderly—elderly people of brute strength. People scratched their heads at the findings. As an old person, I found the rumors offensive. How could they accuse the elderly of doing that to children and helpless girls? It wasn't possible.

I saw him again when I was passing the eateries in front of the market. He was pulling a heavy handcart loaded with tin scraps, computer monitors, broken bookshelves, and construction debris. I couldn't tell that it was him at first because of the baseball cap he wore, but it was definitely him. I strode toward him as if he were a long-lost lover, but I froze. He had stopped in front of a high school girl with long hair. He took out some money from his pocket and handed it to her. With her head bowed, the girl said something and then rushed past the old man. To think he had a granddaughter that age! That's what I wanted to believe.

"I've got to save her. She's walking into the green forest, the evil zone," I muttered, like some hero.

No matter how much I told myself I'd simply ended up there on my walk, I couldn't deny that I'd followed him. He lived on the low hill by the industrial complex. It seemed I had lost my mind. Several huts stood facing different directions on the deserted hill overgrown with weeds. The huts were very small, with Styrofoam or plastic sheet roofs and mud walls lined with flattened cardboard boxes. I walked toward one hut on the right side of the hill that I thought he might have gone into. I don't know if I managed an expression that said I'd gone for a walk but somehow ended up here, lured by the beauty of nature. There was no way to see inside the hut that seemed to have all its windows and door coated with some kind of insulation. Just then, I heard the old man hack and spit out phlegm so loudly that I fell flat on my backside and wet myself.

A few days later, in broad daylight, I went to his home again. Despite the noise from the industrial complex, the hill was eerily quiet. I could even hear in the distance the sound of cars speeding along the overpass. There were no signs of life in the huts. They were absolutely silent, like still-life objects.

• • •

The stench grew worse. They said there may be at least two meters of garbage lying at the bottom of the decaying lake. In every dark corner of the city pooled greenish, putrid water, so there was no escape from the smell. The declarations politicians had made on their vision of building an advanced industrial city vanished. The problem was water. Mothers with young children who'd been drinking water infested with all kinds of parasites blamed the city authorities for their children's health problems.

To top everything off, my toilet broke down again. No matter how many times I called, the rude repairman said he was too busy and didn't come. According to the order of calls received, the earliest he could come was next spring. I called the muscular old man, too, but I couldn't get my spell to work. There was nothing I could do except sit on the floor outside the bathroom and stare at the toilet. Since I couldn't take a dump whenever I wanted, I ate less. I felt bad about emptying my pail on the apartment flower bed, as it was clear that my body was contaminated, just like this city. I had a conscience at least.

There were a lot less people walking around at night. One night as I was coming back from emptying my pail, I saw the old man lifting weights in the playground, seemingly without a care in the world. As though he were a long-lost lover, my entire body began to tingle and all strength seemed to leave my body. But even in the midst of everything, a question lodged itself in my mind: Why would he lift weights here when he doesn't even live in this neighborhood?

It was a theory I couldn't prove, but on the nights he took off his shirt and lifted weights, there was always an incident the next day. The moon shone brightly on the nights he worked out, and after his body absorbed all that silvery light and underwent transformation, he disappeared. Then the next day, the body of a helpless girl would be found. I trembled, clenching my fists. Monster. Evil old man.

"What are you staring at?"

I was so shocked I stumbled back. His voice was commanding, just like his body. Judging by his voice, he seemed strong enough to kill three or four young men at the same time.

"Nothing!"

"Nothing? You've never seen someone lift weights before? How can you say that when you were staring at me like that? Come over here."

I was so scared that I ran as fast as I could. I ran all the way up to the fifth floor. Once inside my apartment, I locked the door. I put my ear to it, catching my breath. Because everything was much too quiet, I couldn't help feeling terrified, but there was nothing I could do. What saved me from the terror in that instant was the smell of something foul.

Excrement had spewed from the toilet and covered the bathroom floor. It had even splattered onto the wall tiles. I started to laugh. I started to understand why my sister had said that I needed to die before her, why she had said she needed to look after me. I could almost hear her voice.

Look at you, look at your shit overflowing like this! Nasty!

Every day I rolled gimbap, as if I were paying penance for my sins. I used the same ingredients as I had done at the gimbap shop. Day after day I ate gimbap, and when the next day came, I rolled more.

A few days later, the plumber came. It took a lot longer to fix the toilet this time. He raised the toilet cover, stuck a long thin metal rod into the bowl, and peered inside. He continued to peer inside, even after the news had covered politics, top stories, and global affairs, and a drama about the secret behind a birth started and ended. From time to time, he answered his phone and spoke to friends who called, even while working hard; it was easy to see he led a diligent, simple life. Was it his last resort? He inserted a metal hose and poured a harsh-smelling chemical into it.

"What took you so long to come fix the toilet?" I grumbled.

"At this rate, everyone needs to become a plumber. A time is coming when at least one person in every family needs to know how to fix the toilet."

"Then what about me? I don't know if I can do that."

He stopped watching the chemical get sucked down and turned to me with a smile. "Don't worry, Granny. I'll come fix your toilet for you as long as you're alive."

At his words, I could only stare at his broad back.

Shuuuuush.

There was the sound of the toilet becoming unclogged.

I put two rolls of gimbap in his black repair bag as he was leaving. His grin made him look foolish. No, he looked adorable. As long as toilets overflowed, he was a crucial member of this society. Plus, I no longer had any family to nag me, even if I had a crush on a forty-year-old toilet repairman.

The next day from early morning, I made gimbap rolls. I steamed the rice and left it out to cool. Instead of tough or chewy ingredients like lotus root, I used shrimp meat, which is easily digestible, and pan-fried the cucumber to make it crunchy. That wasn't all. I ground up walnuts to sprinkle onto some rolls and I even put crushed olives into them as well. The city still reeked, and the stench clung to the ingredients and my fingertips.

I cut up the gimbap rolls and put them in a stackable container. I packed drinks, as well as fruits for dessert, and put them all in a bag. I changed into my workout clothes and even put on a hat. I took a pullover, in case I ended up walking for a long time.

The city didn't seem to be in as terrible shape as the rumors claimed. I walked along the colossal gray bridge and crossed the park with the outdoor pavilion. The industrial complex entrance bustled with workers starting their shifts, and an endless line of trucks raced by.

The hill beside the complex looked warm, having soaked up all the sun. The air also felt cleaner than in the city, but the moment I saw the huts, I was so terrified I began to shake.

I don't remember how I managed to place the gimbap bag in front of the old man's hut. All I know is that when

I made my way out, I was on the main road and I felt as though a big truck had dashed through me. Then I noticed it—the grass stains that covered the hem of my pants.

Radio and River

WHEN HE ASKED HIS FAMILY if they could go on a trip together, they shook their heads, as if to say he should leave
on his own. Immediately, they turned back to the television screen, to the kitchen sink, to the phone, to the doll
that babbled when you touched it. He lifted his head and
gazed out the window. Stretching into the distance was the
forest he hadn't had the chance to properly observe, since
he always left early for work. After taking in the view for a
moment, he raised his arms toward his family, as though he
had something to say, and then lowered them once more.

He walked out into the front yard. He stroked the cat
that was crouching on the entry step. It soon grew bored
and scampered away while he stood staring after it. With his
hands on his hips, he glanced at his house. He turned back
and gazed at the garbage bin inside the fence. After remov-
ing the large pizza box that was sticking out, he folded it in
half and then put it back in the bin. Dusting off his hands, he
turned the baseball cap around on his head, and fished out
his car keys.

The upholstery that had been replaced last summer, the
cookie crumbs the kids had dropped, the rear-view mirror he peered into while picking his nose, the dust particles
floating in the air, the steering wheel and even its distance

to his chest—all these things couldn't be any more familiar. He let out a cough, and as he'd always done, he started the car and set out at a leisurely pace. He'd taken the same route for nearly twenty years, but he found it strange that the same road and the same clouds high above the clear blue sky could look so different. He slowly turned the steering wheel and switched on the radio. And as always, the announcer's soothing, breezy voice put him at ease.

After driving along the downtown border, he crossed a bridge. He soon entered a wide road that led to the factory complex built on the city outskirts. The road was flanked by dense woods. He squinted at the dazzling rays of the autumn sun. Two female students in short jogging shorts ran toward the bridge, soon followed by young men roller-skating to school. A jogger wearing nothing but a pair of briefs also went by, as well as an elderly person with a big dog on a leash. He stopped at a streetlight and wagged his fingers while gripping the steering wheel. The veins on the back of his hand seemed to be trembling and he felt something squirm within him, threatening to crawl up his throat. The muscles in his face felt extremely tense. He grimaced as if sick, and then smiled, and then went back to looking sick.

He raised the volume on the radio. A male vocalist whose defiance had reached a fever pitch screeched, as though intending to eat everyone up. Every time he heard this kind of noise, he felt like his corners had been filed down, so much so that he'd become a smooth lump of metal. But he didn't get angry or feel sick or have the urge to floor the accelerator. Instead, whenever he got in the car, he tuned into radio stations that played hard dance. "To all the listeners feeling down, cheer up!" The announcer's short message sounded like a shriek and the dance beats built speed.

What would his co-workers say if he said he'd rather work instead of going on vacation? He found himself on the familiar route to the factory, rubbing his face and bopping his head to the music. Though he didn't want to go to work, he couldn't think of anywhere else to go. Most of the workers were Mexican, but there were many Asians as well. Unless they had specialized skills, Mexicans and Asians tended to work in the industrial complex not too far from downtown, and he was one of these people. When he first immigrated, he'd also dreamed of working at a university, research institute, bank, or an office job. But he soon gave up that dream. That was only possible in his next life, or maybe the next.

He pictured the faces of his co-workers he would see after swiping his ID card and walking down the hall. He preferred summer vacations over winter vacations. Every summer, his co-workers asked without fail, "Hey Oh, you going anywhere this summer?"

His last name was Oh, but his co-workers found it difficult to say Oh with a short vowel. "My wife said she'll decide. We'll probably end up going where the kids want to go," he'd say, ever so optimistic, picturing himself packing, tuning up his car, and leaving on a trip.

For a while now, his family has been renting the small house along the perfectly straight road in this geometric town. At first, it had felt so surreal to watch people walking along the street that he'd even pinched himself. Back then, the decision to immigrate to this country was progressive for the times, and he'd won the envy of many.

But his family hasn't gone anywhere for the last ten years. In the beginning, they'd gone to local parks and camping sites, and even to lakes and rivers to go fishing. They were friendly with church members, so they got together often with the other families, taking turns hosting. Wearing a floral-pattern apron, his wife prepared dishes, and his kids tottered in the house and yard. But these times were now forgotten. They had been forgotten a long time ago. They were memories stored in an aluminum film can in some corner of an archival chamber. Just like the forgotten reels in cans tagged with illegible dates and titles.

At times he thought long and hard about his family. Though he has written them letters, he has never handed any of them over. With shoulders so rigid they themselves appeared to be encased in a shell, they had an extreme preoccupation with food such that satiating their appetites seemed to be most important of all. Why did they never want to leave the house? He couldn't understand them or himself, or even his cat who couldn't be any more callous.

But something had indeed happened in the last twenty years. There had been a historic flood several years ago. He was more afraid of this flood than the war he'd experienced as a child. He could still smell the water—standing pools that remained in all corners of the city. The entire city had been submerged in water the color of peanut butter. Low-lying buildings along the river, large fields, cattle ranches, gas stations and convenience stores, coffee shops and big-box grocery stores, banks and art centers—all lay submerged. He'd been fine then. But now when he looked at his family who refused to budge from the sofa or bed, he felt as if something darker, something more powerful than this brown water were gushing in. He felt like a child with a hammer who was told to strike either happiness or sadness, and he sensed the hammer in his hand starting to list to one side.

At this hour, the factory parking lot belonged to a flock of small birds everyone referred to as French birds. They were searching for food in the small flower bed in the middle of the empty lot. He heard nothing else, not even the usual ambulance siren, except for the chirping of the birds. He headed for the factory entrance and pushed at the door, but it was locked. There wasn't even a notice stuck on the door. He gave a small wave at the factory, with its asymmetrical overhang and modern silver exterior that looked as if the building were covered with tinfoil.

As he drove east toward the amphitheater, his mood lifted and he tapped his fingers on the steering wheel. The amphitheater's vast stretch of lawn curved gently toward the river. Ahead he saw the bridge that used to be a train track. He rolled down his window halfway. Glancing at the water shimmering in the morning light, he put a cigarette in his mouth. He drove along the river, continuing to circle the amphitheater at about 20 miles per hour.

Dainty flowers that people had brought dotted the cemetery. There were cigarettes and stuffed dolls on some graves. It took a while for him to find Kim's. After hesitating in front of Kim's grave marker, he finally removed his hat, looking solemn, and prayed. He recalled that Kim was from Iri, Jeolla Province. For a long time, he gazed at the gravestone where Kim's name was engraved in large letters.

His body was found in the basement of an art center after the water drained and the building had been standing empty for a long time. Like most of the flooded buildings, the art center hadn't been renovated for over a year, with people restricted from entering. About six months earlier, he'd passed by the center. Though he usually avoided that area, he hadn't been able to that day. The barbed wire gate had been open and the dirt in the flower bed had been upturned. Judging by the rusted ventilators and various objects from inside the building that were piled on one side of the lot, he knew the renovation had finally begun. His heart pounded and he almost tripped over a rock, but his feet took him inside the building. The huge waves had turned the interior dark gray, even the sturdy-looking red brick walls, the long, narrow windows, the arched hallways connecting buildings, and the sculptures and installations placed throughout the center. But the building still managed to look elegant. Before, many local residents had frequented the center, since it regularly hosted children's dance recitals and amateur poetry readings. Unable to walk further into the building, he stood beside a mound of dirt, as if he'd been turned to stone.

No one knew why Kim had been found dead in the cold, dark basement there. Some thought it was the work of hoodlums who'd tried to rob him, but there were no security cameras inside. However, since that sort of thing never happened in the area, the police didn't take the speculation seriously. The investigation was closed before it could properly begin. Kim's wife wailed and could barely speak. Her knees buckled and she collapsed to the ground.

After the funeral, he went to Kim's house to pay his respects. In that short time, Kim's wife had become an ill old woman, and the inside of their house felt empty, as if no one lived there. An elderly white woman from next door who happened to be visiting was talking to Kim's wife.

"I miss my cats, my babies who washed away in the flood," the old woman said, her frail voice trembling.

Kim's wife was clutching a handkerchief, her head bowed. For a long time, their two elderly heads hovered over their wasted laps. He wanted to return Kim and the cats to them, who sat hanging their heads like sinners. Kim's wife couldn't accept her husband's death and kept babbling

some bizarre nonsense to him. As he left the house, he asked
if he could have Kim's cap that was hanging on the wall by
the front door.

From that day on, he took up smoking again. On the
weekends, he and Kim had sat across from each other with
a small table between them, drinking beer and watching sports games. They couldn't quickly recall whether
the other was from Seoul or somewhere in the country.
Everyone at the factory knew Kim as "tall Kim." Because
they were always together like each other's shadows, they
became "Kim and Oh."

He drove around the city all day with the radio on.

The next day again, he got in his car and left the house.
The radio was playing a hip-hop song with long, rambling
lyrics, instead of a fast dance track. Like an actor, the rapper
delivered words like, "asshole, "hell," "pink blood," "cut,"
and "greedy God" in a comic, yet forceful manner. Up ahead
he saw a sign for a rest area and restaurant. He was hungry. A
large artificial sunflower standing by the doors moved its bud
whenever a customer walked in, shouting, "Welcome!" The
restaurant only sold burritos and soft drinks.

He sat by the window. The field across from the road
was indescribably vast. After the flood, many experts announced that water runoff from fields was a major cause
of flooding. Due to excessive land clearing, there was no
vegetation to slow runoff, causing fields to overflow. In the
middle of chewing his burrito, he grimaced and spat out the
maroon-colored beans into his palm. Even the cabbage was
so bitter he no longer felt like eating. After wiping his mouth
with a napkin, he walked up to the servers and handed them
his plate. He told them the beans had gone bad. They apologized with a shrug of their shoulders and tossed his burrito

into the garbage. It landed in the garbage bin with a splat. In a flash, they made him a new burrito with mushrooms.

When he stepped outside, an old man who had been sweeping the front of the restaurant spoke to him. "Have I told you about Sophia? What a lovely creature she was! She was from Russia and she had the bluest eyes and hair so black it was strange. Did you hear? She drowned in the river. Did you know that her father drowned in the river as well? You know the river up there?"

Oh lifted the cap off his head and grinned. Then, ignoring the old man, he took a seat on the bench and smoked a cigarette. He put another one in his mouth after that and lit it as well. Right then, his cell phone rang. Even before he could finish answering, the voice on the other end of the line snapped, "Pick up two half gallons of chocolate milk on your way home," and hung up.

He copied what the voice had said. "Pick up two half gallons of chocolate milk on your way home."

The old man approached him once more and opened his eyes wide. "Hey, do you know this saying? You can't step in the same river twice."

Oh stood up from the bench apologetically and walked away.

The restrooms were located around the back of the restaurant. Instead of going into the restroom, he stood at the bottom of a steep staircase that led up to the second floor. Staring up toward the top, he went up the stairs, drawn by something inexplicable. The stairs were covered with purple carpet, and large black-and-white photos in dark brown frames hung on both sides of the wall at different heights. He climbed to the top, gazing at the pictures. The window at the end of the staircase was wide open and through it, he saw the gentle rolling hill behind the restaurant and the white clouds above. He could even hear the cicadas buzzing. It seemed a completely different world than the one on this side where countless cars sped by all day.

As he was about to make his way down the narrow staircase, he noticed a floral curtain covering a bedroom window. He thought he heard a noise and glimpsed a movement behind the curtain. He moved closer to the window and then stepped back in shock. He cocked his head to the side and looked down at the hill. Unable to resist, he approached the window once more. In the bedroom, two people were making love. He gazed at the man's muscular back and the woman's face coming in and out of view from under him. The woman, her chin slightly tilted up, was gazing intently at the man. For a long time, he watched in secret as the couple undulated together, in time or on their own. He trembled.

There was a lot of traffic along the river, regardless of the season. He wanted to park by the river, but had trouble finding a spot. He and Kim had liked to come here to eat sandwiches and smoke. They hummed along to some tunes and talked about the women they'd known, as if it had happened only yesterday. He managed to find a parking spot and sat inside the car for a few minutes, drinking in the fresh air. It seemed he was starting to feel a little better.

Things were starting to get busy downtown. He parked his car on the quiet side of the road and went into the bar where he and Kim used to go. Everything was the same. The baseball and football games playing on the television screen, even the doll-like server who came to take his drink order. He thought she was pretty with a nicely shaped head. The street outside the entrance was extremely noisy. A group of zombies smeared with fake blood went by, followed by shrieking children. As one of the consequences of being a parent, he couldn't help gazing after them to see if a young Asian was within the mix, but he didn't see his son.

The next morning, he set out in his car again. But before he started the engine, he opened his wallet. After checking his credit cards and cash, he climbed out of the car. He opened his trunk and dusted off his rain boots and running shoes that were tucked away in the corner. There was also a basketball, deflated into a hideous lump. He tossed it into the yard. The cat dashed on top of the ball and sniffed it. After rubbing the dried mud off the running shoes onto the asphalt, he changed shoes.

As always, dance music was playing on the radio. People sent in messages to the station and the announcer read them aloud like poems. When the announcer read the words of one listener who wished for rain, he looked up at the sky. When another listener wished for a kiss, he became self-conscious that his breath smelled like onions from the hamburger he'd just eaten. When still another listener wished to go to Istanbul, he glanced back. He sensed clearly that he was moving farther and farther away from home. A part of the sky seemed to be growing dark, and like a small child, he couldn't help feeling scared, and his head spun, as if he was about to be sick.

• • •

After he'd been speeding for a long time, he saw the river on his right. Boats gleamed under rusty iron bridges. The day was clear without a speck of cloud in the sky. He soon saw a transcontinental train running north and south. He was driving in the opposite direction of the train, but he couldn't see the end. After speeding along for some time, when he was no longer aware whether the train was next to him, the landscape opened up ahead and gas stations and rest areas came into view.

He stopped at a small town near the river. He was very hungry. He saw a post office, church, and motel along the river, the years they were built engraved on the facades. The buildings were a hundred years old at least. He went into a diner connected to a gas station and ate a sandwich and got a takeout coffee. He put a cigarette in his mouth and scanned the town small enough to observe in one glance. Everywhere there were vacant buildings for rent and not a single person walking on the street. He nodded off, sitting on the porch of an empty house with a ribbon tied to its front door.

What woke him was the noise of a passing train. Flies kept sitting on his face and buzzing bees aimed for his face, but he hardly noticed. A bee refused to fly away, too busy sucking the sauce on his fingertip, though he flicked his fingers several times. "Go ahead, eat as much as you want," he muttered, leaning back and closing his eyes once more.

This time, it was a train that went to and from cities in the east. He bolted up from the noise. After straightening his cap, he slowly walked with the river to his right, toward the forked road where the shops were. In front of a bookstore slash library, he gazed at a book poster stuck on the shop window. The faded colors told him it had been up for a long time. The title of the book was Legendary Homeruns. A teen was reading behind the register, his bare feet propped on the counter.

"Can I see a copy of that book?" he asked, pointing at the poster.

"What book?" the teen asked, scratching his head.

He told him the title of the book, but the teen scratched his head again.

"Sorry. We just put up that poster because it was cool. We don't have the book, though."

He wandered aimlessly around the town. The wind coming off the river knocked down a wooden sign on the side of the road. With eyes wide open, as if something extraordinary had happened, he ran toward the sign. An old man who had been dozing on a sofa out on the street looked at him. But he hardly noticed because he'd finally met someone he wanted to talk to—an adorable girl in headphones, riding a bike. Without thinking, he waved at her, but she ignored him and passed him by. "I guess no one likes me," he mumbled. He returned to the gas station diner, and bought two bottles of water, a banana, a bag of chips, and a bag of cheese balls. Outside, the white clouds were turning a little red. He smoked another cigarette.

He sped north in the direction from which the train had come. The sky turned more crimson. He switched on the radio and several songs played one after another, uninterrupted by the announcer's comments. Right then, his cell phone, which he'd left in the passenger seat, began to ring. He didn't answer it. It kept ringing, but still he ignored it. He feared getting addicted to his phone like before. When he'd received the call about Kim's accident, his phone had rung for what seemed a long time. The ringer had sounded unusually loud, too.

On the day of the accident, Kim's number had shown up on his display many times, but he hadn't picked up. He should have answered, but he hadn't felt like telling anyone where he was, even Kim. Everyone was entitled to have a secret or two, he'd told himself. He'd felt a little thrill to think he was someone with mystery. But he could have very well been the last person Kim had called.

"Folks, today's messages are really hot," the radio announcer said with a laugh.

He snickered, too, and muttered, "I like them hot, too."

He hoped he wouldn't have any reception problems. Sometimes there was static and the announcer's voice shook, but it wasn't bad enough to prevent him from listening to the program. A man with a sturdy voice called into the station. He talked about his ex-girlfriend.

The announcer laughed loudly and said the caller's name. "Wait a minute, we've heard this before. You're lying, aren't you? You just changed the girl's name, that's all."

The caller also gave a loud laugh. The story was from a song that everyone knew. He also liked the song, which made him feel a little empty inside. He was probably lonely. He understood the caller. All of a sudden, he lost signal and couldn't hear the rest of the program. He was out of range.

Nine o'clock at night. Trucks with large round flood lights barrelled past. For some reason his body broke into goosebumps and his shoulders flinched. He was very cold. He was hungry, but most of all, he wanted to stop driving. In the distance shone a motel sign that had an angel hovering with outstretched wings.

He snapped awake in the middle of the night, sitting up as soon as his eyes opened. Through the blinds, he could see it was still dark outside. He checked the time. It was only four thirty. He heard a deafening noise then, louder than anything he'd heard before. After using the bathroom, he tried to fall asleep again, but the ghastly noise came once more. This time he buried his face in the bed. And then for nearly an hour, he sat covering his ears with his pillow.

The motel restaurant was open, though it was early. He scanned his surroundings, while having a cigarette. Far ahead, he saw rail tracks going every which way and massive locomotives attached to round tank cars. Only then did he realize he'd come to a kind of hub, a rail yard, where trains were received and sent. The ground was completely black. He walked into the restaurant, had a sandwich and coffee, and read the newspaper. There were several rail workers in uniform, and he felt at ease in their midst.

When he stepped out of the restaurant and was about to return to his room, he heard the train again. He blocked his ears with his hands, but even his teeth chattered. He didn't know how long it took for the noise to stop, but he crouched down on the ground, as if waiting for an earthquake to pass. When he couldn't hear the train anymore, he walked over to the rail yard. The land, slightly sunken, was like a vast sea of oil. The silver train was so long it was impossible to take in its entire length at once. It was bizarre that such a large rail yard would be in this tiny town. He saw more rabbits and squirrels scampering in the woods nearby than people.

He'd never heard of this place that sounded like the combination of unfamiliar French words, and yet, perhaps he'd heard it on the radio. He ambled over to the tracks where the freight cars were gathered. Dark oil seeped out as his feet sunk into the ground. A train arrived right then. Blocking his ears, he ran to a tree and huddled in a crouch, afraid to move. The noise was so atrocious it seemed his ears would start bleeding.

The next day, he could do nothing except worry about avoiding the blast and screech of the trains that came regularly. His daily routine consisted of wandering around this town that had nothing more than some shops downtown by the rail yard and a small residential area. He would start a conversation and then get ignored, try to play with a cat minding its own business, or chase after a rabbit. When he wasn't doing these things, he was covering his ears or his teeth were chattering from the noise of the train, and then he'd realize the day was almost over.

On the third or fourth day, he was surprised to find he no longer had to block his ears at the sound of the train. The noise was relentless, but he could calmly read the newspaper whether the train came or went, but the problem was he never had that day's paper. He thought the town resembled him. A town where nothing happened except the comings and goings of trains.

When he was lounging in bed, an envelope slid in under the door. It was a party invitation to celebrate Gilbert's participation in some war. The street name and number for the celebration were written clearly, and in fact, it was very close by, directly across the street from his hotel. He wondered who this Gilbert was.

The only people at this "party," except for Gilbert who was in a wheelchair, were elderly women with pursed lips, spooning yogurt into their mouths. From time to time, the train went by, sounding like background music, and one by one the balloons hanging from the ceiling popped listlessly. Gilbert wheeled himself over to where Oh sat and shook his hand, giving him a grand welcome. "I'd like to welcome the first Asian to our town!" Gilbert proceeded to tell him about the war he had fought in, but he found the stories so tedious he wished a train would pass by. Right then, an old, heavily made-up woman announced her entrance with sweeping gestures. "Gilbert, congratulations!" Oh was so surprised his eyes grew wide.

The elderly women sat buried in the sofa, staring at their laps, while Gilbert and the woman with the makeup talked to him. The fried chicken and fries she had brought tasted good and the beer wasn't bad either. She handed him a business card. "Do drop by sometime. I think it'll help you."

When the party ended, the woman saw each of the elderly women home. "She's a wonder," Gilbert said to him, who sat smoking in the street.

He nodded at Gilbert's words. He wasn't sure if she was a wonder, but he wanted to say her style for one was something.

"She seems very cool," he said bashfully.

"You sure know your women."

These were the last words that Gilbert said to him, because he never saw Gilbert again.

His body ached from doing nothing all day. Left with no other choice, he went to the rail yard and started helping without a word. Most of the work was to repair and lubricate the tracks. When he finished for the day, he leaned against the stack of wooden posts by the tracks and drank beer. Now that he was using his body, he felt less tired and even his mood lifted. In the evening back at his motel, he looked in the mirror and was so fascinated by the black grease on his face and fingertips that he couldn't help rubbing at them.

Holding the business card the woman had given him, he stood in the middle of the road flanked by about a dozen buildings. Her shop was the first one around the corner from a souvenir shop. Because of the strange letters stuck on her window, he wondered whether he should enter. Right then the door opened and she looked at him with eyes like black marbles.

While she prepared his tea, he sat in a maroon armchair and glanced around the living room. The only decoration he saw were three chairs and a large glass door that covered an entire wall. When she brought the tea, he asked politely, "Are you a doctor? I read the word *healing* outside."

"People said those things, not me. People like you who came to see me. All I did was repeat what they said. Now, if you've finished your tea, please go stand by the glass door. I'll wait for you inside."

The woman went in through the door. Though he couldn't see her anymore, a picture like a hologram kept spinning before him.

"That'll be fifty dollars," she said, as she printed off his receipt.

He became very upset. "But you didn't do anything! All you did was listen to me."

He was furious. She came toward him and kissed him on each cheek. He flinched and stepped back, smelling on her the scent of strange herbs.

"That's my job," she said.

Seething, he came out onto the street. He thought it was time he left this town where nothing happened, except the comings and goings of the train. He smoked in the chair where Gilbert usually sat. After sitting there for some time, he grinned and rubbed his cheek. He packed up his few belongings and checked out of the motel. The nightly price of the motel was so cheap that his entire one-week stay cost very little. He walked out into the motel parking lot and started the car.

• • •

The art center doors were open and he heard voices from inside the building. When he walked down the stairs, he saw two men in coveralls standing right up against the wall, scrubbing its surface. Tangled wires hung down from the wall and the air reeked of chemicals. They were art conservators. He asked if he could look around and they said yes. They were restoring a mural—a strange mural they didn't know who had painted or when it had been painted. In fact, it had only been revealed when the flood had ruined two layers of the exterior wall. The half-human, half-beast characters filled one end of the mural to the other. These creatures were human with animal legs and horns on their heads, and some had faces that looked like that of the Buddha. The mural even depicted the boiling waters of Hell.

"Isn't it amazing? We have no idea who drew this."

The mural filled the entire wall all the way up to the ceiling, except for a small gap in the center. And through this opening the size of a door, he saw the cold, damp space where Kim had been found.

He couldn't recall the exact spot. Because the basement didn't get any light, it was hard to tell which was the wall and which was the floor. He stepped toward where he thought Kim had been lying. All of a sudden, he felt a chill and the smell of dirt pricked his eyes. Clenching his teeth, he covered his mouth with his hand. "When will the restoration be finished?" he called out, taking a few more steps forward, but there was no response. He walked closer toward the wall. Through the crack in a small window, white light streamed in. In the light were two chairs and seated in one was Kim. He took the chair next to Kim. Kim offered him his hand, which he clasped. Kim smiled and he did as well. "Did you have a nice vacation?" Kim asked. "Of course," he replied, still smiling. Slowly he began to tell him about his dull trip, how he'd stayed in a town where the only thing he'd heard was the relentless train.

Death Road

It was H who told me about one of the most danger-ous roads in the whole world: Bolivia's Yungas Road. After graduating from university with a civil engineering degree and completing his military service, he worked at major road and tunnel construction sites all over the country. He had been my soccer buddy in elementary school. On some days after school, just the two of us would stay behind on the soc-cer field, kicking the ball around. The male teachers heading home would tease H for playing soccer with a girl. But not once did H look down on me because of that. We would walk home eating ice cream, watching the sky redden above the bridge.

Several years ago, H was appointed as the manager of a toll gate in Gyeonggi Province, and since then, has hand-ed out 10,000-won highway vouchers to everyone at our year-end reunions. When there was a lull in our conversa-tions, he'd tell us about the vehicles that would get caught on highway security cameras. The footage captured by these 24-hour cams was analyzed daily by the staff. This always proved to be a scintillating topic for a group of elementary school alumni now past their prime. The tales of what would happen on the highway—especially on rainy days—were so entertaining that H wouldn't share his gossip for free, at least not without someone offering to pick up the tab at the next bar or throw in a gift certificate.

On an ordinary evening last spring, I went to see H while he was having a beer with his colleagues after work. When I look back, it was rude of me to intrude. But I needed to be with somebody that night. Maybe because of this uninvited guest sitting alone in the corner looking glum, his colleagues slipped out one by one. Around midnight, only H and I remained at the bar where the shadows of artificial cypress leaves shook on the plaster walls. As we drank our beer, I found myself getting emotional and got up to go to the bathroom. I took my cell phone with me and stayed inside the bathroom for a long time. When I finally came out, H was still there in the same spot.

"What's wrong?" H asked.

H looked the same as he had when we were just kids playing soccer, except he was now wearing glasses and a suit. I felt strange. I probably said I was feeling a little blue and that was when he told me about Yungas Road.

Who knows why a bank would carry out research on the world's most dangerous road? A Latin American bank named Bolivia's Yungas Road "The Most Dangerous Road in the World" that year, the reason being that ever since it was built in 1935, more than two hundred people had lost their lives on the narrow switchback each year. Like other treacherous mountain roads, this one was also built by prisoners of war, and it was said that many of their bodies lay there.

Apparently, the waterfalls that gushed beside the highway disoriented drivers. After driving through heavy mud and fog, barely making it out alive, drivers veered off the road on blind corners and plummeted over the edge. As the road that connects the Yungas and La Paz, one of Bolivia's largest cities, Yungas Road was undoubtedly perilous, but the view at around 4,500 meters presented a massive river meeting the Amazon. For anyone with a driver's license and thirteen-plus years of driving experience who's looking to meet their end in a car, Yungas Road was perfect. This is what H said.

H lived in Gangnam, but that night he insisted on accompanying me home, which meant that he had to go all the way around downtown Seoul. Near Seongbuk-dong, as the road rose uphill, he answered his phone and talked quietly with his wife, covering his mouth with his hand.

"Yeah, with people from work. I'm on my way home. The kids asleep?"

Listening to her voice coming through the phone, I gazed out at downtown Seoul, at the city seeming to sink deeper into darkness. When H hung up and cracked open the window, I grabbed his right hand, which was resting on his knee. I didn't think anything of it and was merely treating him as I always had when we used to play soccer together, but he kept clearing his throat, as if uncomfortable. I'd been out of line once again.

It's not that I lacked the opportunity to attempt suicide until now. Two years ago in the fall, I had gone to China. If I think back, it had been the perfect time. If I had the same strong desire then as I have now, I would have carried out the act without any obstacles and disappeared for good. Cable cars that transported you up a mountain for an hour without a safety belt or safety net, precipices where a single misstep would send you tumbling down a deep canyon and cause you to never be seen again, highways where trucks barreled past you at 150 kilometers an hour like bullets.

After flying for four and a half hours, I'd landed in Kunming of Yunnan Province. There was no grand purpose for going on the trip. Several girlfriends happened to suggest a trip to China, and it just so happened that there were many backpacking trip promotions to China around then. I felt fine when we were visiting historic cities, like Dali and Lijiang Old Town. Lijiang Old Town, with no city walls and its streets dating back to the Qing Dynasty, was incredible. The waterways led right up to people's front doors so the city was nicknamed the Venice of the East. If you stood at the corner of an alley where weeping willows swayed, you felt as though someone you longed to see would come walking toward you at any moment.

However, the morning we were supposed to go up Jade Dragon Snow Mountain, considered by locals as the symbol of Lijiang, my stomach began to hurt. Even Lijiang was 2,000 meters above sea level. As soon as we got off the bus at the cable car station, the girl with altitude sickness started sucking back bottled oxygen, while I winced from the pain in my stomach. The other members of our party glanced at us as if we were pathetic. At more than 5,500 meters above sea level, the mountain, which was the southernmost section of the Himalayas, remained snow-capped all year round. They claimed Jade Dragon Snow Mountain was magical. Whether it was true or not, something spewed from my stomach each time I opened my mouth. It came out the other end as well. With my pride in tatters, I ended up being admitted to a local hospital. After examining me, the doctor said: "Congratulations on becoming the first patient in Yunnan Province to contract SARS."

He was joking, but it seemed SARS would hurt less than what I was experiencing.

"Maybe you'd better return to Seoul," the guide said respectfully. "It won't be easy to keep traveling in this condition."

It seemed the girl with altitude sickness and I would have to pack up our things and go back home. I also didn't like the way the young guide was acting polite all of a sudden, as if he meant to distance himself from me. I could find no reason to go back, except that I didn't want to take powdered medicine. At the hospital, I'd learned the medicine didn't come in capsules, so I needed to mix the powder with water and drink it like a protein shake. I vowed to hold out.

"I'm okay going anywhere as long as it's not Seoul."

At dawn the next morning, doubled over from stomach pains and the invigorating sound of sweeping coming from the square, I boarded an old van that looked as though it would fall apart any second, along with the guide and girl with altitude sickness. The girl had a Filipino boyfriend, so she kept making long-distance calls to the Philippines every chance she got. For her, talking to this boyfriend was a reason to live, so I followed her around and sometimes even translated for her in my broken English.

Until that point, I had no idea where we were going or what we were seeing. The rest of our group had already gone on to Zhongdian, our final destination. At last, they reached that magical place—Shangri-La. But we never did. The only things I remembered from that time were the colorful clothes of the country women and their rotten teeth when they opened their mouths and laughed. In those uncomfortable clothes, the women picked tea leaves in the fields until the sun set.

The road was dangerous. The guide who had seemed mild-mannered turned out to be extremely adventurous. He took us on a test run of a route his tour company was developing. He was the only person we could rely on. We had no choice but to look to him for everything, since we couldn't possibly negotiate the car fare with the Chinese drivers on our own. There was no winning against them. After climbing out of the car for a moment to look at various animals for sale on the side of the road, one driver started the engine and took off. Or after we had told another driver our destination and pre-paid our fare, he stopped by the homes of friends and relatives, and even his workplace, as if it were the most natural thing in the world, and once he'd finished running his errands, finally set out for our destination. In the end, we just had to laugh.

The rough road continued. We left Lijiang and passed through Zhongdian, heading north. An alpine area at least 3,000 meters above sea level, there were landslides everywhere along the way. Occasionally we encountered gorgeous views that resembled what I imagined paradise to look like, but it was impossible to relax because the constant rattling and shaking from the bumpy road made me dizzy. The mounds of dirt that blocked the road, countless mountains and paths, racing along endlessly in the six-person van—they drained us. The other girl became too exhausted to even think about calling her boyfriend. As for me, all distracting thoughts left my head. We finally stopped at a village where small cement buildings were clustered together by the road.

"See? I knew you would like Lhasa."

"Are you saying this is Tibet?"

We were so surprised we couldn't shut our gaping mouths.

"We're actually in Tibet?"

"You sure have a great feel for things."

To be exact, we weren't in Tibet but at the juncture of Yunnan and Tibet called Diqing, known as "Little Tibet." It's said that the famous Ancient Tea Horse Road began there. It got its name from the trade practice of Tibetan ponies in exchange for Yunnan's tea, but I had no idea at the time. Our lodgings were uncomfortable, so I slept hunched over. We were so dazed and hungry we could have eaten a car. On a hill in the middle of the market where Buddhist monks walked to and fro, we filled our stomachs until they threatened to burst. Even while we ate, they stood behind us, bowing toward the snowy mountain towering above the plateau.

"That there is Meili Snow Mountain," the guide said.

"Another snow mountain?" We kept eating.

This I also learned later, but if we had gone further north, we would have reached one of the two most dangerous roads in all of China. Apparently three thousand young people had died to build the 2,000-kilometer road that ran west from Chengdu, located in the Sichuan Basin, to Lhasa at 4,000 meters above sea level. Frequent landslides and tortuous curves, a constant lack of oxygen. I can't help thinking that I should have done whatever I could to get on that road and die there.

It had started one ordinary morning when I walked past the Gwanghwamun intersection toward the entrance of Samcheong-dong. I was wearing flip-flops and thin black cotton trousers I'd bought from Indonesia and had a heavy camera dangling from my neck. I had gotten enough sleep, so I felt more energetic than usual and was in a decent mood, too. It seemed that if I stepped onto the path to Samcheong-dong up ahead, a green forest would appear and the tiny plane hovering over the forest would throw open its door and wait for me.

One block behind me, in the new wing of M Gallery, the work of a German installation artist was being exhibited.

A blank guestbook, which no one had yet signed, caught my eye. I picked up a pamphlet, folded it into a square, and put it in my bag. The scale of the exhibition was impressive. Giant plants in glass boxes faced the floor, its leaves and roots rubbed with bits of iron, gold, tin, and lead. For some reason, my skin crawled looking at it up close, but from far away, it looked almost magical.

I went into the coffee shop on the first floor of the gallery and ordered a coffee. The espresso machine was so loud that I had to turn away and look out the window. A shuttle bus came to a stop just then and expelled a group of Chinese tourists in dull clothes. Chinese words spewed from the tourists and invaded the street. A guide holding a flag stood at the front and slowly led the group to Samcheong-dong. The machine stopped its noise long after, when I'd been staring into my mug for some time. There was a small whirlpool in the center. I bit into a cookie, and as it slowly dissolved on my tongue, something swept through me. It was from this point that I became gripped with depression at all hours of the day.

The rainy season was coming. Each night the mugginess flooded into my room. All night long, the local girls practiced for the newscaster exam outside my low-rise. Clear, high-pitched voices chirped constantly about recent diplomacy and trade issues. I had to eat something, but I had no appetite. The packs of Chinese herbal medicine my mom had sent me were turning to ice in the freezer, still in the case. She'd used the money she'd been putting away little by little to get the moles removed from her face. The soybean paste I had bought a long time ago had long expired, the leeks and spinach had turned to mush inside the newspaper, and the eggs had gone bad.

Every morning and every night, I checked my email. Among the spam, an email requiring my immediate action caught my eye. It had been sent by library circulation services.

The following checked-out materials are coming due. Please return them by the due date. Barcode: MV03411 × Across a Gold Prairie (DVD) × Borrowed date: April 15, 2008 × Due date: April 22, 2008

It was a Japanese movie about an eighty-something-year-old man who believes he's still young and falls for his new housekeeper. The girl, who makes Japanese pickles in a red plastic container, seemed like a real housekeeper. Unable to distinguish between dream and reality, the old man climbs onto the roof at the end and jumps, not believing what he was experiencing is reality, and ends up falling to his death. It was a bit sad when the lead actress sobs and says, "I'm scared to be happy."

Maybe the DVD was buried in some corner, but I couldn't find it. I couldn't even recall the cover. After turning my home upside down, I received a very strange phone call.

"Sis, I'm in Busan. I went for a swim this morning and suddenly didn't feel like living anymore, so I did something bad. I went out really far. I'm a mess right now. The coast guard had to give me CPR."

I hated the expression "of a different mother," so I sometimes used the word "step," but anyhow he was my stepbrother. My dad, before the age of fifty, tried to kill himself and neatly pulled it off. His friends said it was better this way, better he did it in one go, rather than making a mess of it and ending up in intensive care. Since my mom and my stepbrother's mom were rivals, neither of them attended the funeral. So it was my stepbrother, in his junior high school uniform, and I, in my senior high uniform, who quietly stood watch at the hospital funeral home. We took the meager condolence money, paid for the expenses, and left for the crematorium. Once we were done, we transported the ashes to the columbarium and then took the bus back to the hospital, getting off in front of the main gate. My stepbrother carried Dad's funeral portrait. Having taken care of everything, we stared across the street at McDonald's. We each ate a hamburger and parted ways.

After that, we called each other only when there were major changes in our lives. Before, I wouldn't have been so shaken up by that kind of phone call. I'd been someone who lived with two feet planted solidly on the ground, never once dreaming of escaping this life. In fact, I'd been more sensible than anyone, renting an apartment near a subway station for convenient transportation, using term deposits to save money, collecting overtime pay, and splitting the bill when eating out. But now, all these things that had been a matter of course felt like someone else's business. Plus, it didn't feel good to learn that another person who shared the same blood suffered from the same illness.

The DVD was nowhere to be found. I gathered up the pile of papers, books, and movie pamphlets on my desk and tossed them. There was a bundle of ribbons I'd saved from boxes and presents and I tossed that as well. Never-worn dress shoes, sneakers with ripped seams, even heavy hiking boots—I tossed them, too. I even got rid of mementos, traces of other people. T-shirts with familiar designs, handkerchiefs and belts, popular books, and even fish sausages full of preservatives. They had belonged to K, the guy I'd dated when I was working as a temp for a telecommunications company. Back then, the stress from the day had melted away at the thought of someone waiting for me at home, peering out the front door. But rather than melt away, more things began to weigh on me as time passed. I experienced another breakup for the umpteenth time.

I paced around my small apartment, but no appropriate tool caught my eye. Just as I'd suspected, I wasn't the type to carry out the deed at home. Around then, an elementary school friend's mother passed away. At a hospital funeral home in Pyeongchon, we two women and six men stayed up all night. Starting with beer, we moved on to soju, and then back to beer, and then to soju again. Our eyes became bloodshot, turning red like those of rabbits. The subject that night was the best way to make a lot of money, live a comfortable life, and then kick the bucket. One friend talked about an accident he'd seen on the way to the hospital—a 10-car crash that had happened around 8 p.m. in heavy fog and light rain. The road had looked as if it were suspended mid-air and all you could see were a few neon lights sparkling faintly in the distance.

"Who saw *Blade Runner*? It was like a scene out of that movie."

"This guy watches a lot of movies, huh?"

No one else seemed to have seen the movie.

"I almost crashed into the car in front of me."

When someone said Gangbyeon Expressway was the most dangerous road in Seoul, H added, "We call it 'Death Road.'"

I felt sober all of a sudden. By "we" H meant professionals like him who dealt with roads for a living. I took out my notebook and pencil and started taking notes. Every word that came from H's mouth seemed like a proverb.

At daybreak, friends who had to go to work headed to the sauna to wash up and I went home and slept all day. When I awoke in the evening, I opened my bag and checked my notes. Nothing else was particularly important, besides "Death Road." If I couldn't go to Yungas Road and if I couldn't go back to China, it made sense to pick a road close to me as my final destination. All of a sudden, I became energized and was glad that I knew how to drive. I turned on the computer for the first time in a long while. Of all the spam emails, the one from library circulation services felt the friendliest.

The following checked-out materials are overdue. Please return them as soon as possible. Note that a fine of 500 won per day will be charged from the due date until it is returned. Barcode: MV03411 × Across a Gold Prairie (DVD) × Borrowed date: April 15, 2008 × Due date: April 22, 2008

• • •

They say a person contemplating suicide usually warns someone of their despair. I was thinking of informing the library circulation staff member who'd sent me the email. *Hello, I'm thinking of killing myself today. I'm unable to return the borrowed item, so please purchase a replacement.* I wondered if a message like this would cause a big commotion in a quiet library, and grew curious about the librarian's expression. But where the hell was the DVD? I had no idea where it was.

According to the results of a study conducted by the Seoul Expressway Traffic Management Center, the section between the north end of Han River Bridge and the north end of Dongjak Bridge had the highest accident rate. In the past three years, there have been 66 accidents per kilometer. When I went onto the Seoul Expressway website, I could see in one glance Seoul's vast highway system. The map, flashing to indicate congestion and accidents, was adorable. In the middle of the night if I shut off all the lights and stared at the screen, the city of Seoul seemed like a toy. Covered with dainty warning lights, the entire system blinked like a heart, with the Incheon airport on the left and the Hanam Junction on the right, the Surak Underground Roadway above and the Yangjae Interchange below. When there was heavy rain or fog, many accidents occurred, so the whole map became full of wounds. With Mount Namsan situated right above, I could almost smell the trees, their fragrance wafting down to the accident-prone north end of Han River Bridge and the north end of Dongjak Bridge.

The first day was no good. Maybe I was a little flustered, because I hadn't taken out the car in a long time or maybe I'd chosen a wrong time, because the roads were unusually busy. After leaving the Gangbuk district and passing through downtown, it took a long time to get on Gangbyeon Expressway. I wore a pair of white gloves, scared to feel the blood on my hands once I crashed, though one of my biggest pet peeves was drivers wearing white gloves.

Was it around Yongsan? I stopped to pick up a coffee from Coffee Bean. When I returned with my coffee, a security guard was glaring at my car with his hands on his hips. As soon as he saw me, he yelled at me, stomping his feet.

"Move your car!"

I suddenly became so angry that I couldn't help raising my voice, too. When I realized he hadn't said "please," I grew more upset.

"Don't yell at me! Who do you think you are, yelling at me?"

If there was another thing I hated, it was people who got into fights with building security guards. Because what did they ever do to anyone? But why were all security guards so pigheaded? You could never win with them.

When I finally managed to get on Gangbyeon Expressway, it was unbelievably hot and congested. Lunchtime traffic filled stretches of road with long queues that I couldn't find a suitable place to step on the gas. Clear sunny weather was not a good condition for doing the job. I was so exhausted that I passed out as soon as I got home, even though it was broad daylight.

After checking the weather forecast, the second day I picked was dark and cloudy. The overcast day exposed all the problems with the expressway. First of all, the sign for the highway entrance was so confusing, and the merge lane was too short. It seemed a collision was going to happen any second. However, it wasn't my job to come up with ideas to improve road conditions. Anyhow I managed to get onto Dongho Bridge and sped toward Banpo. I turned on the radio out of habit. I followed the flow of traffic, and tried taking my foot off the brake and flooring it. In my own way, I was trying to finish the job. I was concentrating will all my being, from the top of my head down to my toes, that my whole body was tense. My car might have been old, but I even heard funny noises from the engine and loud clunking from time to time.

Just when I was growing used to the situation, the cars ahead came to a standstill. I had to get from Dongjak Bridge to Han River Bridge, but everything was backed up. I turned off the radio. I was angry and frustrated, and the view across the river on my left felt surreal. I rolled down the window. The traffic sounds were something. Drivers smoked, their left arm sticking out the window, or talked on the phone with earbuds plugged in. They were always on their phones—in traffic and even when they were racing along. That was it. Using the phone was key.

I connected my earbuds to my phone and started looking through my contacts. Since we were going at a crawl, I had no problem looking up a number. Actually there was no reason to look for it, since I knew it by heart. It was K's number. Instead of saying "hello," he said nothing. Annoyed by the traffic, I didn't have the patience to be nice.

"You can't even say hi?"

At my attack, he remained silent. Right then, the cars that had been creeping along at 30 kilometers an hour began to speed up and a hot breeze swept in through the window.

"You don't even know how to say hi, you jerk?"

Did everyone become aggressive once they sat in the driver's seat? He heaved a sigh and said, "If you're going to be rude, I'm hanging up."

When he responded so arrogantly, spouting a cliché line straight out of a movie, anger shot through me. The car ahead was moving farther away and was about to enter Dongjak Bridge.

"Then hang up! Hang up, you asshole!"

The asshole then actually hung up on me. As soon as the line went dead, I floored the gas pedal like an enraged bull. I flew down the steep section of the highway under construction, even managing to change lanes. If I carried on in fifth gear and crashed into the pier, it would all be over. Not only would there be at least a four-car or five-car collision, but I would be smashed into smithereens inside this old car. I couldn't wait.

But in my hesitation, I ended up passing the construction zone altogether and my car hurtled along as if it meant to keep going all night, past Mapo Bridge, Seogang Bridge, and Yanghwa Bridge, even to the ends of the earth.

On the day of my third attempt, it rained. To be perfectly honest, I wanted it to be like a scene out of *Blade Runner*, so I picked a rainy day on purpose. For the first time in my life, I filled the whole tank with gas and even fired off an email to library circulation. I'd taken care of everything.

If there's a 20-car collision on Gangbyeon Expressway on a rainy day, it'll be a total disaster.

The words I'd heard at the funeral gave me energy. "I guess today's the day." The voice that rang out in the car sounded like that of a middle-aged man.

I gripped the steering wheel. I was wearing white gloves again. I took my time getting on the Mapo Bridge. The rain was causing a traffic jam. If I wanted something to happen, I needed to speed up, but I couldn't go any faster. It was much easier to drive standard when you could go fast. If not, you needed to keep shifting gears, which wasn't easy for someone like me with weak arms and legs. The swish of the wipers, the radio, and the whirring of the engine made me sleepy. I kept nodding off. If this continued, it seemed I was definitely going to get into an accident.

I kept touching my cell phone. In the end, I called again. At first he didn't pick up, but when I called about twenty times, he finally did. Nothing was moving anyway, so I pulled up my parking brake and talked. It was K this time as well.

"What did I do? Why are you doing this now?" he asked, sounding exasperated.

"You have no idea, you jerk?" I couldn't help blowing up at him, and the rain came down harder. Because of the sound of the wipers, I had trouble hearing him.

"I know I'm a jerk, but what are you doing? Aren't we finished?" he asked.

"Yeah, we're finished."

"How about working on yourself for a change? How are you supposed to meet someone nice if you keep acting this way?"

This is the way he was, addressing you in a condescending, mocking tone, eventually making you doubt yourself.

"You called because you miss me, right? Then why don't you try being nice?"

"What the fuck? You think I called because I wanted to see you?"

The second my voice went shrill, the line went dead.

"Piece of shit!"

I felt like crashing into the car in front of me. I was speechless. Tears sprang to my eyes. I couldn't even shift gears. I wanted to die, but even that I couldn't pull off. I had set out to die, but I couldn't explain how, in that moment, I wanted to ask someone to save me, to tell someone I was struggling. The rain kept falling and the world across the river looked positively apocalyptic. I ended up pressing H's number on speed dial.

"What's wrong?

I was sobbing so hard that H could tell immediately that I was crying. He seemed to be at a restaurant. I could hear music, voices, and the clattering of dishes in the background.

"I'm on Gangbyeon Expressway. I think I'm going to die. Can you talk to me?"

H sounded different, which shook me, but I tried to keep my tone lighthearted.

"I'm scared I might do something I'm going to regret!"

"Then stop the car!" he snapped before I barely finished getting the words out.

"How? I can't!"

"Turn on your hazard lights."

"I said I think I'm going to die!"

"Stop the car! Why can't you stop the car?"

Though he was telling me the safest course of action to take, he was getting angry at me.

Can't you see you're ruining my relationship with my wife right now?

He didn't say this, but I could tell that I—a single woman, someone he'd known since elementary school—was disrupting his family dinner. I wanted to say: Maybe you shouldn't have been nice to me from the beginning, you asshole.

H made me angrier than my ex-boyfriend. I hung up, not wanting to hear dishes clattering. I had no idea where I was, but I started to speed. The friction between the rubber tires and the rain-slick pavement traveled up my thighs and the sound of the wipers was like music. The inside of my head bleached white and things that had felt snarled seemed to come untangled, and I found myself saying in a husky voice, "Forget it, you shitheads."

I rolled down the window and spat onto the sizzling expressway. The blinking clock on the dashboard was just passing 9 p.m. I found myself passing the on-ramp to the Dongjak Bridge. There was no traffic, so I didn't have to go below fifth gear, and though it was night, white clouds hung brightly in the sky. The moment I passed the Banpo Bridge on-ramp and then the Dongho Bridge on-ramp as well, I glimpsed the inner ring road ramp leading to Uijeongbu. Getting on the inner ring road was very dangerous. I could hardly see anything through my rear-view and sideview mirrors. Cars zoomed past. Freight trucks weighing 4.5 tonnes roared by and only after they had passed did I feel the reverberations. No one let me in. Everyone raced along at a breakneck speed.

When I entered the inner ring road going toward Seongdong, traffic was hurtling past at full speed. It was quite a distance to the Gangbuk-gu Office exit. I'd finally learned to get home to Suyu-ri by taking Gangbyeon Expressway, getting onto the inner ring road, and then going by Gangbuk-gu Office, instead of cutting through downtown.

When I got home, I checked my email. My message to the library had failed to deliver, since it was a send-only email address. I boiled some instant noodles and watched television. My gaze fell below to the TV stand and there behind the glass door, tucked neatly between my books and DVDs, was the library DVD.

Disaster Area Tour Bus

I STARED AT THE THERMOMETER for a while, unable to tell if what I was reading was Celsius or Fahrenheit, and in the end, simply dashed out into the street. A real scorcher, where the sun prickled the nape of your neck from morning. It sizzled at midday and a hotter breeze blew in the evening. But if you woke in the middle of the night, the air was chilly enough to give you goosebumps. One winter, someone had stuck snow down the back of my neck and fled. I felt as if that cold lump of ice was still there, stuck under my armpit beside my breast. Once again yesterday, I didn't call my mom. My dual time zone watch indicated it was early morning in Korea. It was around when she would be sitting before a mound of spinach spread out on the newspaper, shaking dirt off the stems.

Street artists set out their work and tools and said good morning to those walking by. Tour horses with colorful headdresses dozed on the road. One serious fellow, who never joked around, asked, "If you were born again as an animal, what would you be?"

"A horse," I said without thinking.

It was what I'd wanted last summer, to gallop away and kick whatever I felt like kicking. My tanned face was full of sunspots, and in my bag were canisters of undeveloped film full of desolate images. After work, people poured onto the streets, as if they'd all made prior arrangements to meet. Highschool girls climbed onto the roof of police cars and raised their fingers in peace signs, snapping pictures of one another with their digital cameras, while I followed them and clicked the shutter on mine. One day someone hollered at me from behind. "Hey, young man. Can you take a picture of that?" I turned to see where he was pointing. People were being beaten by the police. When everyone swarmed, water cannon trucks came and parted the group in two with their blasts. The police dragged them off by their arms and legs, and trucks continued to spray water at the crowd. Everyone retreated, taking cover behind the subway station or an obscure building. I followed them to the station and caught my reflection in the bathroom mirror. My T-shirt was soaking wet, sagging like a potato sack, and my sneakers were filthy beyond belief. But how could he mistake me for a young man? It was insulting, but it was true I looked awful.

I spent the whole summer on the streets and, one night, when the entire city gathered on the street, something hit me on the head and I collapsed in a corner of the plaza. A scuffle had broken out between the police and the people in front of me, but it wasn't serious enough for the batons to come out. But I'd been knocked in the head by something. Since it was impossible to catch a cab there, I dragged myself past the plaza all the way to the tunnel entrance. I managed to get home and was nauseous for several days. Summer passed and winter came.

It's been one day since I arrived in this place that's considered the best tourist city in the country. The ground around the old cathedral was brown and parched. The air reeked of cigars and oysters. I knew almost nothing about the city's history that dated back hundreds of years. All I knew was that it was first founded by the French, ceded to the Spanish, and then returned to the French. I stepped on crushed ice cream cones, colorful feathers that had been stuck to party masks, cigarette butts, and crumpled flyers that littered the sidewalk.

Several homeless people tottered by, clutching plastic bags. They loomed close and shoved me in the shoulders, saying something I couldn't understand. I gave my fiercest frown and barked, "What did you say?" They seemed to be asking if I had any cigarettes, but when I turned around, they'd disappeared. The words that had gushed from their deep, dark mouths were either too slow or too fast. Sometimes their words sounded like a rhythm without meaning. Another homeless person came up to me and muttered something. When I asked if she'd had breakfast, she shook her hand at me. I didn't know if she understood my question. I handed her a bill. She seemed neither grateful nor sorry, just a little surprised, and put it in her plastic bag. When I had gone to a Southeast Asian country where the soil was red, little girls had followed me everywhere, begging for money. I glimpsed anger in the eyes of the small boys, who had followed me a long way to sell me a single book. That country had been poor and this country was wealthy, but there were many homeless people here. The aroma of coffee wafted out from the café across the street and spread through the alley.

I jaywalked across the street. The tourists sitting on the café patio said good morning to everyone walking by. I said hello as well, but I couldn't muster a friendly expression. How could they smile and look so cheerful, sitting on a patio at such an early hour, calling out: "Hello!" "How did you sleep?" "What beautiful weather we're having!" and "Have a great day!" How could they exchange these greetings and start the day so gaily? The people I knew wouldn't be able to do it. Where I was from, we always got yellow dust in the spring. There were no disasters, but we lived as though there were. People got sick and killed themselves and became enraged. Even when winter came, snow didn't fall, and having lost the memory of white snow, we welcomed Christmas as acid rain fell. Those who experienced these infuriating things traveled to the sea to watch the first sunrise of the new year, and with their entire family packed in the car drove straight into the sea. Endless self-torment, humiliation, and self-loathing drove both young and old to climb to the top of high-rise buildings and jump. Tormenting oneself turned into tormenting others, and new incidents broke out every day and old incidents were quickly forgotten. So frequent were these things that we couldn't catch our breath. The more people gathered in the plaza, the taller the concrete barrier on the road got. People scrawled graffiti on the wall. *What are we doing here? Didn't the Wall come down a long time ago? What the hell is this?*

And yet, why did this city, which had experienced a major disaster, feel so alive? The breeze blowing in from the Spanish-style building carried the smell of warm brown sugar. The sound of the bass trombone came from the French quarter. I felt as if dark sugar was dissolving on my tongue, and I didn't mind the air that seemed to be browning my body. A man in a black vest walked toward me. He placed a café au lait and a dish with two beignets on the table and left. A strong gust of wind sent the ends of the tablecloth flapping and the powdered sugar from the beignets scattering in all directions. All at once, a flock of birds swooped down and pecked at the crumbs on the ground. I envied them.

I glanced across the street. A group of tourists was standing in front of a hotel built a hundred years ago. The balcony with the wrought iron lattice was lovely and people inside the dazzling entrance were playing cards, even this early in the morning. Though an airport shuttle arrived, the passengers standing outside seemed unconcerned and kept talking with one another. A woman climbed onto the bus, but it didn't leave right away. A set of drums, saxophone, bass, and keyboard passed in front of the bus, heading toward the café. They were a family street jazz band. The son looked like his father and the daughter looked her brother. While they set up for the performance, a large crow flew into the café. The tourists screamed and another gust of wind blew. My clothes and bag became covered with powdered sugar. I couldn't wipe it off with a wet nap and I couldn't blow it off either. I only seemed to be working the damned powder deeper into my clothes.

A red streetcar running along the harbor sped toward me, ringing its bell. No one got off and no one got on. A bus was standing in the vacant lot by the streetcar station. I was sure it was the tour bus I was supposed to get on. I got my ticket at the little kiosk facing the harbor. Music drifted out from a docked dinner cruise. The boat rocked gently in the water, a banner hanging above with the grandiose words: *Dinner performance, unforgettable moments on one enchanted evening.* Why did I feel dizzy whenever I saw a boat, even when it was moored? Bile would come up if I so much as looked at one. I recalled the first time I'd been in a big city. It had been in Korea, and I'd gone looking for someone with an address in hand. When a large crowd of people had surged forward at the crosswalk as if en route to some urgent appointment, I'd suddenly felt nauseous. As if someone were cramming a drug down my throat, a drug that would drain all my strength. I'd tried to cry out, but no one had noticed. The city I'd seen that day had also rocked like this boat.

Thank y'all for joining us on the Disaster Area Tour bus today. We're gonna be cruising about three hours, but don't you worry none about getting bored. Now if you need anything—some water, a pit stop, a little charge for your cell phone—just holler and I'll take care of you. We're fixing to hit the road real soon, so buckle up for a wild ride.

The bus was packed with tourists of all ages. There wasn't a single empty seat. The Black bus driver went down the aisle, asking each person where they were from, and even saying hello in their language. He sat back in the driver's seat and started the engine. Then, as he spoke his opening words into the microphone, the tour commenced. Going on guided city tours was one of my must-dos when traveling. The first thing I did, whenever I visited a new place, was to look for a guided city tour. A tour of the same area, depending on whether it took place during the day or at night, was completely different. On one tour, in some European country, I'd boarded a bus and was surprised to see it packed with so many gorgeous men. But I learned soon enough that it was a tour for gay travelers. The ticket agent back at the kiosk had asked if I'd be all right. I laughed belatedly on the bus, realizing what she'd tried to explain to me. Those dazzling young people had really been something. I couldn't recall anything, except the men's high-bridged noses and exquisite faces, so it was safe to say the tour had been a waste of money. I'd even been on a suicide tour bus, like the one from the Japanese movie *Suicide Bus*. But rather than looking somber, the people on the tour had laughed and talked and kissed. In fact, they'd looked happy to death.

The bus quickly made its way onto a boulevard. Large supermarkets and burger joints with familiar names whisked by. With a large industrial district looming in the distance, we crossed a bridge. Even after we'd crossed it, the view of the factories didn't disappear from the windshield. The driver continued to speak in a dialect peculiar to this place. The people in Gwanghwamun Square last summer had also spoken in a dialect. We'd talked while staring each other in the face, but we couldn't understand what the other was saying. Everyone grew angry and beat their chests and chanted in a language only they knew. Babies in strollers snatched at protest candles and shook them. Dialect. Dialect everywhere. People were asserting themselves in the same language, but it couldn't stop the summer war. No one could go home, and they circled the streets all night long.

It went down on the last Monday of August. In the wee hours of the morning, it came busting through this city square. When I peeped and saw them lights shining bright in the dead of night, I was so shook I hopped right out of bed. Now some folks already done left on account of the storm, but some stayed, you know. They were too poor with no cars to make a run for it. Can you imagine living in this country without a car? We had no rides to load up our stuff and split.

It be a spirit, a mighty wind that swirled round the square. It got bigger and bigger, like it was going to blow. If it ain't no spirit, then how'd it do what it do to this city? Everybody, take a look to the right for a sec, that's the famous NASA Michoud Assembly Facility. Ain't it ironic it's sitting right here? Anyways, that morning the wind came howling in like drums beating. Suddenly I recalled what my mamaw used to say. The scariest thing in this whole wide world is the cough of an angry sea. She must have seen some spooky stuff too. If she was still kicking, she would have smelt the hurricane from a mile away. Oh, I sure do miss her.

The city sucked up all that wind and rain, like a scene straight out of those disaster movies you watch in the summertime, and now the whole damn place was sitting underwater. See the Superdome on your left? A "refuge of last resort," they called it, but later on, papers said it was a big old mistake to put folks there. And that statue of the man on a horse? He was a hero in a famous battle and the seventh President of the United States! But the hurricane done busted up the statue real good. Now we're heading to the area with the most damage. By the way, ain't we enjoying some gorgeous weather today? Just look at the sky!

The vast sea gleamed outside the window. The road ran along the water with hardly any coast. Lovers kissing with the car door wide open, women reading while sitting on a bench with their feet hooked to strollers, the back view of three elderly people in a neat row of camping chairs, gazing at the water with outstretched legs. The scene was so tranquil it felt unreal. Whenever I looked upon a peaceful scene, it seemed to be part of my DNA to superimpose miserable images over what I saw. Hideous images became superimposed over a relaxed, happy landscape. Shards of glass, blood dotting my white sneakers and the cement floor, skin stinging as if I'd been sprayed with salt, cows stumbling and dying, a long mirror showing the backs of cancer patients, people burning up in flames, women wailing, acid rain, and my body scattering in all directions. Last summer, I'd been sick, so sick that I felt as if I would shatter. Maybe that was a bad habit of mine. An old habit of crying bloody murder when I wasn't actually sick, screaming and wailing, just so that I'd feel alive.

Now y'all, look to your right. See that lake? It connects to the canals running into the city. You know the National Guard pushed the floodwaters back into the lake by piling sandbags in the canals?

When the flood came, the Virgin Mary statue in the convent court-yard was the first to go. That convent's in a low-lying district, you know. Those damn cars were next. And then guitars, trumpets, pianos, tables, farm equipment. All in a blink. Water the color of peanut butter rushed into the city. Single-story houses, two-story buildings, even little churches went under. My dear friends and the white sisters at the convent who helped our poor Black folk and the women I loved—they must have been scared witless, scrambling for their phones. I can still hear them. The terror, the screams nobody heard, the brown waters that swept in and paralyzed you, the despair... But don't y'all be sad like me 'cause this here's just the Disaster Area Tour bus.

The words spewed out of the driver. Moved, the passengers cried, "Oh!" and "Ah!" and listened intently.

I barely made it out alive. Ain't no other way to describe it. Eighty percent of the city went under and we were scared out of our minds. We climbed up on our roofs and huddled under blankets, praying for the water to go down. When our kinfolk and friends slipped and struggled in that nasty, muddy water, all we could do was holler and cry. That's what we did all week—holler and cry. What else were we supposed to do? You goddamn hurricane, you nasty, vile thing! That's all we could say. But you know what broke my heart? The cats and dogs, they vanished just like that, like they'd all left on a trip together. But some were slick and survived by hiding in the bathroom sink. Now we're moving on to the parts that got tore up real bad.

An old woman from northern Europe dabbed at her eyes with a handkerchief. The faces of all the passengers were somber as they listened to the driver's monologue.

The bus moved to a residential area along the coast, traveling in the outside lane, going right by the single-story houses that lined the street. It was a large residential neighborhood, but even in the middle of the day, not a single person could be seen walking around on the street. Chairs with broken legs sitting in front of houses, serial numbers painted on the outside walls, skulls and crossbones symbols on the porch, roofs blown off, smashed windows, houses tilting as if about to fly away.

You wanna hear what was in the paper then? After the hurricane hit, plenty of folks skedaddled. They said they ain't never coming back. One third of the city dead, gone, or missing. Houses were abandoned and nobody tried fixing them up. Those dreadful memories chased folks away for good. They ran off, ditching everything, never looking back.

We stopped in front of the abandoned houses that had been damaged in different ways. The driver had many stories about each house. It didn't matter if he was making them up. The passengers sat up, leaned close to the window, and snapped pictures. I sometimes pressed the shutter, too. Every time I heard the shutter, I flinched.

After last summer, I'd stopped taking pictures. I no longer wanted to make money that way, and I didn't like telling people that I was a photographer. But he had liked me, a photographer, and I'd shown my work only to him. After making love, we would use a magnifying glass loupe to look at my negatives. Country roads in Taiwan, endless pastures in New Zealand, cold eerie industrial landscapes in England. Then we came to the ones of Gwanghwamun Square. Images of people being beaten and dragged away by the police. He grabbed me and sat me on his knees. "We really need to get rid of these people," he said. "They make a goddamn fuss about everything."

We broke up soon after. When he asked why, I said it was because we didn't speak the same language. He told me to grow up and stop acting like a child. He said adults didn't break up for that kind of reason. My mind felt clear, but my body throbbed with pain. I felt as if I'd come apart at the seams, so all day I wrapped a blanket around me. On a plane or on the street and even inside a public bath, I needed to keep something wrapped tightly around me. From that point on, I no longer wanted to take pictures. I lost my magnifying glass, and I drank and swore and got into fights with people.

I caught the words *2 dogs, 1 cat,* and *Help!* on the wall of a house.

Lemme tell you about this house.

The bus crept forward, stopping before a house where the front and back walls were missing.

You see the missing wall back there? A woman lived here with her two boys. She worked all day, hustling to send them to school. She couldn't evacuate 'cause she was more worried about losing her job. To put her boys at ease while they were away at school, she wrote a message on her roof: Mama is alive. *But sadly she died. They found her wedged in the back door there, her body all puffed up from being in the water. Do you know? For generations, we were slaves. We earned twenty dollars a month, with names and ages you could barely recall. Go on down to the museum next to the parish and peep for yourselves. They've got newspaper ads for slave auctions from those times. What did that poor woman ever do to deserve this kind of fate?*

The bus moved at a steady speed. A strange hush fell over the bus. The mood was very different from when the tour had first started. The driver spoke faster and faster. How painful it must be to re-enact those memories. I gazed at his reflection in the mirror above the driver's seat. But what was this? He seemed very excited.

All they did was go around in boats, handing out water and blankets to folks stranded on rooftops. The military choppers came in, dropping watches, water, and sandbags, but it wasn't enough. Reporters from around the world rolled up here, but ain't many folks come to lend a hand. Did you know our president was at his ranch at the time and saw the hurricane only through satellite images? What if the spirit had paid a visit to another city instead? Enjoying a fancy New Zealand lamb dinner with his pals, cracking crude jokes—that was our president. By the way, I heard critters in New Zealand get exposed to this poison called 1080. What if a sheep that ate the poison got slaughtered and ended up on the president's table? Ain't it enough to make you break out in a cold sweat? Anyways, this country is one great nation, don't you think?

A week after the hurricane hit, the floodwaters started going down. They said it was gonna take about three months to drain. Everything was pure chaos, you know? Painful to walk around. Houses, the skyline, telephone poles—all smashed up. Vintage clocks scattered across the road, signboards cracked, banquettes turned upside down, everything pancaked. My daughters' school got knocked down, trucks rammed into the ground, houses were plucked up and torn apart. The crematorium, the graveyard, the tombstones, the flowers—everything was topsy-turvy. Cars full of sand lined the streets. The whole city was broken. The Superdome, our last resort, and even the big theme park, once the pride of this city. The boats docked near the canals crumpled like paper and dead fish floated up, showing their pale bellies. The streets turned into graves for refrigerators, cars, and furniture. Oh, this street here is where a lot of musicians have their studios. We're gonna stop for a bit.

I made out some faint letters on a wall: *8 cats, 2 dogs, you rotten hurricane, go to hell!* There was some graffiti of a trumpet.

After the water drained, you know what we laid eyes on? The pitiful bodies of our neighbors. Every time they moved a body to the

*tent that was a temporary morgue, we stood up and howled. The
musicians who survived covered themselves with blankets and played
their instruments while shedding tears. That's how we expressed our
grief. It was our prayer and incantation. All we could do was sing
and cry and join the procession along the river. In the end, we had
no more tears. It was our custom to play upbeat jazz and laugh
when folks we loved departed this world. We always sent them off
with laughter, but this time, nobody did.*

*Folks are still gripped by fear. They haven't been able to move
on from the pain. Go give the downtown streets a whirl. You're
gonna witness plenty of wandering souls, souls that have lost their
minds from the trauma. A buddy of mine went wild, roaming the
woods and rummaging through abandoned fridges to find his. Elders
struggling with respiratory issues, skin ailments, cataracts. But maybe those things ain't so dire as children losing their voice and women
their smiles. Many are suffering from anxiety and depression. They
can't erase the image of those bodies. Ah, I'm being too solemn,
ain't I? Why don't we take a little breather before we carry on?
Here we go, we're turning right into the park now. Oh, you see that
straight ahead? Those big old trees with leaves resembling Papaw's
beard? They're what we call Spanish Moss, the symbol of this city.
We'll take a little break here.*

The trees, covered with what looked like drooping
white beards, sparkled like some fairy-tale country at dawn.
I saw white doll-like children playing on the lakeshore by
a flock of ducks. An elderly couple whispered lovingly to
each other under an outdoor shelter with skinny pillars, her
back against his chest. I also saw teenage boys chatting, toss-
ing whatever they were holding into the air and catching it
again. When the wind blew, the leaves covered with white
beards hung down and shook softly, and for some reason,
I felt as if those leaves would land on my head, so I kept

looking up. A grandmother and a little girl were playing under a tree, holding hands. "A white hand is going to come down from the tree and snatch you away," the old lady said. The girl screamed and ran away. Beyond the far wall of the park, I saw the cool sky and the sea. It was hard to believe a tidal surge from this picturesque sea had created rain, over-flowed canals, and swallowed up the city. All of a sudden, I was thirsty. My heart started racing and my neck felt stiff. The little girl who had been with her grandmother ran toward me. I called out to her, and she seemed to glance at me for a second, but ran toward the lake, her golden hair streaming behind her. My eyes stung and I was exhausted. One by one, the passengers who'd been standing at the rest stop climbed back onto the bus.

Have y'all tried our ice cream—the pride of this great city? It's simply sublime. I bet you ain't ever tasted ice cream this good. Now why don't we mosey on out of here and keep going? Oh, looks like some Spanish Moss got stuck on the roof. Hold on and lemme work my magic. Ah, there we go. If y'all look back at the park for a sec, you'll see where they set up the volunteer camp. Did you know it was countries poorer than ours that sent the most aid? It ain't our government or the military that saved us.

Then one Saturday morning, the water drained away and the sun rose like nothing ever happened. Folks gathered on the steps of the square, their bodies ragged. The roads around the city reopened, and everywhere on the promenade, on streetcars, we saw the words: We Survived. *There were messages on shop windows too.* September 11, a girl was here until Friday. I saw her make soup out of her own dog. *Or* We overcame hell. *Or even:* Don't touch me, I'm sleeping. *Clear, short sentences, like poetry.*

Check out this residential area. This here took the worst hit. At the time, all the street signs pointing this way were smashed up.

Like the gods themselves were saying heading east was a bad idea. But look at the houses now, they're looking mighty fine. The state's redone them. Those telephone poles you see over there got knocked down and tents filled every lot.

There were "For Rent" signs in front of the empty houses.

"Did people come back to their homes?" someone asked.

The driver shook his head from side to side, saying nothing. We'd seen no one else, except for a few cats and a man riding a bicycle with one hand while wheeling another bike. I saw a boat parked in an alley, as though it'd been carried there on the floodwaters. The rusted yellow boat was sitting at a strange angle on the property that was as desolate as the sea.

That Saturday night, downtown was a warzone, folks screaming and fighting over relief items like it was the end of days. Wrapped up in Russian issue blankets, they gathered in front of the distribution center. I was lucky enough to find a case of canned tuna and was sharing it with my neighbors, so I wasn't there to see it. If I was there, I dunno what would have happened to me. They ran out of supplies real quick and folks started fighting, but nobody knew something so awful was about to go down. Things spiraled out of control. The next day, the National Guard came in to stop the looting. Many of them had just come back from fighting a crazy war in another country and now they were here in our city. There was no money to rebuild this city 'cause the government poured it all into that damn war. In their dark sunglasses and military uniform, the troops marched into the city center and grabbed Black folks by the collar.

All right, y'all ready to drive on in? Well, things got worse. One hot afternoon, a fire started smack dab in the city center. It went bang and a huge pillar of fire shot up into the sky. Fire trucks and the National Guard rushed in, sirens blaring like crazy. The troops were exhausted, trying to put out the fire, but folks just lost it and attacked them like they were possessed. Bottles and garbage went flying, but they didn't back down. After that, Black folks in the disaster zone were labeled as plundering villains, and the next day, the National Guard took over the entire city. We had no power to do a damn thing. From that day on, the city walls were filled with writings about looting and death. It was hell on earth.

You're looking at the sea from the other side now. Ain't it something beautiful? The National Guard, they beat down Black folks like there was no tomorrow. But we didn't back down, no sir. Some even fired back at them. White folks couldn't understand why we'd shoot at soldiers and sided with the government. The hurricane, well, it was no longer the main issue. Rioting Black folks became the focus. We were poor, too poor to evacuate. All that rage we'd been holding in for so long, it just exploded. The strength of our rage was mightier than any hurricane. How could a hurricane, how could any natural disaster, be so cruel? We cried, we laughed, we screamed. For many years, experts have been warning this city was a disaster waiting to happen, but nobody did a damn thing. The president was out there playing golf and the government was busy spending money on some stupid war. One government official said: My honest assessment is that this government does not have the sufficient finances to cover the cost of damage restoration here.

I still dunno how we made it through all that. A couple of months passed. Folks gathered at the harbor, cutting each other's hair and lining up in front of ambulances to get medicine for their skin troubles. We got some therapy, too. Everyone just stared up at the sky. Time kept on going and Christmas rolled around. It got cold, and to get supplies, we wrapped ourselves in blankets and made a long line stretching from that city park we were just at all the way to this beach. You see this spot right here? This is where we stood. The beach was covered with paper plates. There were piles of them everywhere. They symbolized our emptiness. Oh, what a terrible sight it was. Dirty shoes, kids' backpacks on the ground, starving cats and dogs, these poor souls with nothing but sorrow. We didn't want much, we just hoped folks would help. Folks who wouldn't oppress us or beat us, folks who would quietly give us a hand. The new year came and January rolled in. Time kept on moving. The sea, the canals, the lake had the gall to look calm and peaceful, like the hurricane was all a lie.

The bus was crossing the bridge that led into downtown. There were passengers who were nodding off and others I made eye contact with who appeared a little dazed. We started to run into some traffic once we crossed the bridge. We went down a street lined with antique shops, galleries, and restaurants. The driver's commentary had stopped by now. In the air, I smelled the city's signature aroma of brown sugar. The bus let us off in the middle of the city and we dispersed very slowly.

Gumbo is a famous local dish. With a map in hand, I walked down blocks, circling the city, and finally went into a restaurant that didn't look too busy. It took almost an hour for the food to come out, but I didn't get angry. After I left the restaurant, I gazed blankly at the darkening streets. In this city, many people ask you questions. They ask if you could break a bill, if you have a lighter, if you were Chinese. Back home, I also asked the grannies at the market a lot of questions. I asked about a ring a granny had on her left hand, and I bought the soybean sprouts and grain they displayed before them. I loved walking in Samcheong-dong in late summer and I loved the narrow alleys that split off and came back together in front of the Jeongdok Library and cheonggukjang restaurant.

A white man approaches me and starts talking to me. He says he likes Asian girls and asks if I have time. I say I do, but that I'm married. Then he asks where my ring is. When I say I left it at home, he says I'm lying and asks me to come back to his place. "I'm nice, good-looking and I have a house," he says, spitting as he speaks. I grin and turn away. I smell the cloying odor of liquor on him.

The darkness grows deeper, but the lights are very bright. Everyone is happy and lively. Men swarm toward the adult shops, women show themselves to the men for a second and then rush back into the shops to hide, drunken men piss in the streets and are arrested by the police, and those who have painted themselves with metallic paint stand frozen as live statues. All the shops have their doors thrown open, and laughter and people dancing spill out into the streets. Various music mixes together to create a jumble of beats, and the night is a hodgepodge of people and pavement.

I'm on my way to an old venue where a famous jazz musician, born in this city in 1901, used to play. The year the shabby concert hall was built is branded above the entrance, where a crowd is already waiting. I purchase a ticket and head inside. It's dim inside and the ceiling is low. A few benches are set up in rows. A broken fan sits on top of the piano and there are four scuffed-up instruments covered with stickers. The performance hasn't started yet. I step out into the hallway and look around. The musicians are standing behind a barbed wire fence marked with a "no trespassing" sign. They drink water and talk on the phone. Moments later, a child holding a Black man's hand opens the fence door and walks out onto the stage. People sit on the benches and many more stand in the back. The audience consists of different nationalities, relationships, and ages. A glib host comes on stage to introduce the band. The musicians are all old like this concert hall, except the man in the black shirt—the one who had walked out with the boy.

When the performance starts, people begin to move their shoulders without a word. Gradually they clap and shake their heads to the beat. As the night continues, the hall grows darker, more crimson, in color. Each piece is different, and even the performers take on different expressions every second. Here, familiar tunes I'd heard on CDs sound like new songs. The camera flash goes off and several people walk up to the stage to toss some bills into a basket. One man limps to the front and starts to swing dance. As the night grows deeper, people become more and more captivated by the music.

The child who had been watching the performance climbs into the drummer's lap and begins to play. He strikes any drum he feels like. The drummer, who's missing a couple of teeth, plays along, keeping in time with the child's playing. They're in perfect rhythm. The musicians laugh. They sing and laugh, as if their ancestors had never been enslaved, as if they'd never experienced a hurricane. They open their mouths and laugh, like people who play a jaunty tune at the end of a sad and solemn funeral. I follow along and open my mouth and laugh.

Near the end of the performance, the musician who'd come out with the child gets to his feet. His lips close around the mouth of the trumpet. The first low notes ring out.

Back in 1963, a famous musician from this city had visited Seoul. When he was a child, his father had abandoned the family, and the boy had been sent to a juvenile detention center where he learned to play in a band. He'd never had his own Christmas tree until the age of forty, and though he'd given joy to everyone, he'd been treated like a minstrel. The band was playing his song, "What a Wonderful World."

Greenland

AFTER DATING A TOTAL of three men my whole life, I married the third one. Whenever I mentioned this, my rude co-workers covered their mouths with their hands and pretended to gag. "Manager, how can you tell such a lie?" How could I have dated only three men my entire life? To be honest, it was a little unfair. But there was nothing I could do about it now, like the fact that the sun rose from the east and set in the west. It was the truth. I'd been with only three men.

The story I'm trying to tell has to do with the third man—my husband. Or to put it more grandly, I'm trying to talk about the crisis the world faced at the time, the kind of things my children ate, TV shows that were popular. Or maybe it'd be better to say this story is about an earring I lost—an earring I had no idea I'd even lost in the first place.

He was always surrounded by friends, so naturally after we married, I saw them, too, from time to time. Though they were young, they owned a gas station, seafood restaurant, convenience store, and so on. Even if their official titles were *department head* or *director*, they were essentially CEOs. When they got together, they usually played pool or cards, and turned to hard liquor as the night progressed. They usually wound up at a room salon at the end of the night, despite their insistence they'd only gone to a karaoke lounge, and the exorbitant bill was always divided equally between them.

"But they're their own boss! Why couldn't one of them pay for the whole thing?"

If I said anything along these lines, my husband just grinned and said, "They're selfish bastards, that's why."

Then I'd pout and move onto the next question. "So what do you do at a room salon?"

"Pretty much everything you can imagine," he said, blowing on his nails he'd just filed.

He must have thought I was stupid. But it was true that my knowledge about room salons was limited. I asked him repeatedly what the inside looked like, but he refused to tell me. In the end, unable to withstand my tickling and nagging, he offered one detail. "There's a pole. And someone hangs from it." Consequently, I believed men exercised at room salons. "Ah, so you exercise while you drink!" I'd say, full of curiosity. But he continued to cut his toenails without bothering to look at me.

He'd been an average student at a high school notorious for having a heavy workload. He was honest, having grown up without ever worrying about his tuition, with frugal parents who always had a hot meal ready for him. There was nothing secretive or underhanded about him. And you could tell how easygoing he was from what his mother said, as well as from the flatness of the back of his head. "What kind of baby just eats and sleeps and eats and sleeps? He never cried. All day, he lay quietly in one spot. He basically raised himself."

Even after marriage, he was considerate enough to let me keep working. What I mean by *considerate* is simply that he never told me whether I should keep working or not. While

I worked late several days in a row because of a special anniversary event, collapsing into bed without having the energy to wash up, he would come home even later and drink wine or another can of beer before heading to bed, as if he had all the time in the world. Watching him, I knew I couldn't keep up. I realized then that this would be the story of our marriage. There would be no changing him.

Amid all the busyness, we wanted to grow our family, so we tried our best, but what could we do? We encountered difficulties. "It seems you have a low sperm count," the urologist pronounced. My husband went on medication to increase his sperm count, somehow managed to quit drinking, and even stopped seeing his friends for a time. Thanks to his efforts, our first child was born—a Gemini, when the air was hazy with yellow dust.

While we bought a compact car and made monthly payments on our life insurance, my hair style changed according to the fashion, from tight curls to stick straight, a short bob to loose waves. Pregnancy and childbirth broadened my back, but I continued to work. Like us, his friends started to have kids as well, and our gatherings naturally turned into first birthday celebrations. At the end of the party, we pushed our strollers to a barbecue or soondae restaurant. The men stood around the strollers and talked, letting the wives enjoy the rare night out. We sat at the table, knocking back shot after shot of soju, and whenever we stepped out to visit the bathroom, the twenty to thirty empty soju bottles lined up in the gravel yard fell over with a crash. On our way back from the bathroom, we staggered toward the strollers to shake our heads and coo at our babies. They looked up, babbling incoherently at the mommies, whose eyes were smudged dark with makeup, who'd tried desperately to hide the love handles bulging below their blazers.

After discussing which of their homes would be able to accommodate all the moms and kids for the night, the men called a few taxis. Once they'd stuffed the strollers and drunk women into the house, they dusted off their hands and finally headed off for their pole exercise. While we mixed spirits and beer and took shots, the babies pawed at their diapers or grabbed the hair or face of the kids lying next to them. Who knows where all the baby back ribs and pork belly we'd devoured at the restaurant went? We ordered tangsuyuk and stir-fried seafood and vegetables. As long as the toddlers didn't slip on the peanuts scattered across the floor, hit their heads, and get carted off to the emergency room, the night was a success. We spent most weekends this way, or in the complete opposite way, lounging the entire day in bed.

Even when the economy got so bad that there were rumors the country needed a bailout, these gentlemen were fine. No, they were better than fine. They earned more money, in fact, by making high-risk investments. It was actually a few years later, when those risks were gone that they started running into trouble. No one knew why. It was a time when oil companies were raking in money because of fluctuating oil prices, but somehow the gas station owner was the first to go out of business. He had so much wealth, however, that he was able to set up a new business right away and maintain the title of CEO. One friend, a director at a mid-size company whose stock price hadn't gone up or down since going public, moved to a remote city where an office building appeared after endless stretches of farmland, and became the director of a smaller, similar company. Another friend, the CEO of an apparel company with several large retail stores, couldn't last two seasons after laying off their design chief, so he had to close half of his shops, but at least he remained the president. Compared to these gentlemen in fancy suits with well-pressed pleats and bespoke Italian shoes, my husband and I were ordinary office workers with little money and little family backing. It was around that time that we, with the least promising futures, were held up as having the most stable jobs. When he'd first told them he was marrying a woman two years his senior, an ordinary office worker who had graduated from a trade school and was the daughter of a family with no money, his friends hadn't understood. "What's the matter with you? Why are you doing this?" they'd said, pinching him. They believed that people working in art and culture tended to suffer more traumatic events in childhood or were from a fringe group. But when they began to experience problems themselves, we were re-evaluated as people with a great philosophy and deemed experts in the culture sector.

Around the time our daughter started talking, my mother, who'd practically raised her, grew frail and ill. Despite always claiming that the stress of looking after our child would send her to an early grave, that she'd probably croak while washing dishes, she urged us to have a second child. I lamented the foolishness of women. The pain of childbirth and mastitis had not yet faded from my mind, and I hated to turn into a beast again, but the queen of the kitchen sink kept chanting: "Just have a boy. I'll do everything then." I don't know why this sounded like begging to my ears. Plus, my husband and I'd been saying we wouldn't have any more children, because of his low sperm count and because we hardly made enough money. But my firstborn was a Gemini and true to what the sign suggests, there must have been a cherub roaming the sky each night, wondering where to deliver the next bundle of joy, because how else would we have gotten a second child? Never in our wildest dreams did we think another baby would be in the cards for us. What my mother wanted was a boy. Not having a son had been her complex all her life, but how could she put that on her exhausted daughter? At first, it seemed her wish would come true. But contrary to her hopes, the moment I felt the little nugget hovering over our house slip into my body, I sensed it was missing the object between the legs that my mother desperately hoped for. It was a girl.

Around this time, my husband's friends began borrowing money from each other. Maybe he didn't want to upset me when I was pregnant, but he started taking his calls outside. Occasionally, when I spoke with the other wives, they talked about how someone was having a hard time, or that someone's parents had sold their home—things concerning real estate sales and minor investment failures that were hardly newsworthy. It just sounded as if they were getting a smaller slice of the pie.

It was also around then that the company I worked for experienced great difficulty in securing donations. An overseas business founder, who had made a generous donation every year, died from an illness and we received word that the new management would no longer be pledging their support. According to the senior staff, we could expect a certain amount of foreign donations and aid before the Seoul Olympics, but a foreign organization was unlikely to give money when the average annual wage in South Korea was so high. We put our heads together to come up with next year's funds, but all we did was drink.

Regardless of our situation, the baby completed her ten months in the womb and came out into the world. With a back as broad as a wrestler's, minus the baby weight, I returned to work once again. In the absence of large-scale donations, the only way to raise funds was to reach into people's pockets, but the hardest thing in the world was to make them open up their wallets. There were times we would host an event, only to have reporters attend, and in some cases, the weather and even the catering were disappointing. When the economic situation was bad, everyone flocked to the public service projects of local agencies, trying to get a piece of the budget, so the only things that increased were phone calls and haggling with officials. Meanwhile, I tossed back many shots, and for better or for worse, I lost weight without trying.

Christmas went by while the news said a crisis could be an opportunity, that the economy had hit rock bottom, as if they had agreed in advance to spew the same reviews and predictions. My husband's friend, an executive for a department store, threw a bash for his mother's seventieth birthday. In the basement hall around Seolleung station, we saw one another for the first time in a long while. Some of our children could now eat on their own without our help, and they sat at their own table in bow ties, shouting "Cheers!" and raising their glasses of coke. As her son's friends came in droves to congratulate her, the birthday girl kissed each friend in excitement, danced, and enjoyed herself. The event started at three in the afternoon, but by nine o'clock, the stale air of the basement hall turned everyone's eyes bloodshot.

The men waved at the elderly woman, the star of the night, until her car carried her away. Then they went outside and stood smoking around an ashtray. Unable to find a suitable place in the neighborhood where they could pack off the women and kids, we all headed to a bossam restaurant nearby. Under the bright light, everyone looked a little different. Their faces seemed somewhat dented, they'd grown a little shorter, and they didn't talk as much as before. Even though their kids had fallen asleep next to them, the men smoked and snickered, telling the same stories from high school that they told every time they got together. Right then, one of my husband's friends said to me, "You've lost so much weight I almost didn't recognize you." From that point, they started teasing me, saying they needed to address me more respectfully, since I was an "older woman," or asking if they could see my ID—things they said to me whenever we got together. Then one of the wives, who had been sitting in the corner drinking shot after shot of soju, started to cry. It killed the mood, and we became so flustered we didn't realize the stew on the portable stovetop was boiling away. Her husband, a CEO who was doing very well for himself, escorted her outside, and the rest of the men hung their heads and smoked. The night ended in a bizarre way. Now looking back, it was the first time they didn't go to their "pole" club.

Winter dragged on without giving us any opportunity to savor the snow. I was hula-hooping when the cries of the first babies born on New Year's Day were broadcast live on television from maternity wards across the country. I grew a bit sentimental, thinking of time passing and all the new babies being born. I sprawled stomach down on the bed and opened my journal, trying to record my New Year's goals and resolutions, but for some strange reason, whenever I took up my pencil, all I could do was record how much money we needed. It wasn't that we were living beyond our means, but things were tight and our debt was growing. Still, we weren't in big trouble yet.

I went to my oldest child's kindergarten class for a parent observation, and the sight of my daughter raising her hand at the teacher's question made my heart leap, as if something grand had happened. *She's earning her keep at least,* I'd thought. If it weren't for these small joys, it was hard to be in one's late thirties in Korea. Whenever I met unmarried friends who'd studied abroad in England or America and claimed you needed to invest in yourself the more uncertain the economy was, I felt an unbearable pain. Forget about studying abroad—I was struggling both at work and at home, and my unhappiness was only growing.

Then something happened. During a period when the only emails I ever received were bills and spam, when my reading consisted of documents, contracts, reports, and pamphlets, rather than proper books, I received a message I'd desperately needed. It was an email from an elementary school friend whose face had instantly come to mind as soon as I read her name. Through that popular alumni search website, I'd gotten an email that began with: "I miss you, old friends." I wondered how this friend had gotten my email address, but I realized once more that it's always your own doing. Once when I'd been bored, I'd registered myself on the alumni site and created an account. It seemed ten other classmates had created accounts as well.

Just as people said, the elementary school reunion was fun. The fact that we could call one another by name and talk comfortably without regard to gender or interests was fascinating. But for better or for worse, we now get together only if something bad happens, like for the funeral of a parent. But do we still have a good time when we get together? No. It isn't easy to find a time to meet and not everyone comes out anymore. Now I can't even remember my ID and password for that alumni site. At first, everyone had sparkled, but the more we met, the more we talked about our problems, it was tiresome to talk about the same things we always talked about. There was one who always complained about their hard life and one who always boasted, and even the restaurant menus seemed to repeat themselves.

I'd heard about people losing a lot of money in investments, but until then, no one I was close to had experienced something anything serious. Then late one night, the wife of one of my husband's friends called. Once we'd asked after one another, she said they'd had to downsize because of failed investments and that their marriage was also on the rocks. She let out deep, long sighs, and her voice shook with anger. She mentioned she didn't think the men saw each other much anymore. "They're just old friends, after all."

I wasn't sure, since my husband didn't tell me every single person he met with, but hung up, after saying weakly, "Wouldn't they keep seeing each other, since they're good friends?"

Then a week before the Lunar New Year, my husband went to meet his friends for a game of cards. After washing up the kids, I lay down and was about to read through all the old newspapers to catch up when my landline rang. Sounding completely sober, my husband asked me to bring the car right away to a restaurant nearby.

What greeted me was a scene out of a Hong Kong noir. Even the name of the restaurant—Busan Restaurant—was fitting. The owner stood in the kitchen with her hands on her lips, glaring at the customers who'd turned her restaurant upside down. These sharply dressed men leaned back in their chairs and smoked. One of them, a former taekwondo athlete who'd always boasted that he was good at fighting, clasped his right fist that was wrapped in a white cloth with his left hand and spat repeatedly on the restaurant floor. His moussed hair gleamed, and his shirttail had come out from his trousers. Shards from a broken mirror glittered on the ground, and who knows how it had happened, but the surface of their table was clean, while plates and beer glasses were strewn across the floor.

I guessed the friend with the injured hand had broken the mirror, but I couldn't tell who else was hurt, so I merely looked at my husband without saying anything. As he did when he was nervous, he kept blinking his big eyes. They lounged back in their seats with their legs stretched out in front of them. Then one of them sat up and said with a grimace, "The gap between the actual and ideal is getting bigger, you idiots."

I didn't understand what he meant, but it was the same friend whose investments had tanked. While the owner griped about how these men were making her lose business, one kept spitting on the floor, and these gentlemen, who occupied the whole restaurant, made no move to leave. I knew what I had to do: pay the bill and escort the men out.

"Please, you don't have to do that."

While I fumbled for my wallet, the one with the failed investments pushed me aside and got to his feet to go to the counter. When both his credit cards were declined, he bowed his head and heaved a deep sigh. He turned around all of a sudden, and with everyone watching, hurled both cards down on the ground and stomped on them. While the rest of the men swarmed to the counter, I took out cash from my wallet and took care of the bill.

The mood inside the car on the way to the emergency room was awkward and silent. I turned on the heater, only to turn it off, then turned on the wipers, and raised and lowered the volume of the radio. In order to lighten the mood, I even fiddled with the tuner dial to switch to a different station. Neither my husband nor his friend who had injured his hand said anything, so I had no idea what had happened.

The emergency room was so packed there were cots placed in the hallway and hardly any room to step inside. We waited a long time beside an elementary school student who was suffering from severe abdominal pain. Because there were no empty beds, we watched her run frantically to the bathroom a few minutes after she'd been given an enema. Even at that hour, the mother jabbered on the phone about how she'd had to bring the child to the ER in the middle of the night because she'd been complaining of stomach pains, that her rectum was full of shit. "Shit, huh?" my husband's friend said. We snickered. The emergency room late at night was something to behold. While we waited for our turn, the pink stain on the white handkerchief wrapped around the friend's fist spread, turning darker, while the street outside disappeared in the thick fog.

My work life wasn't particularly great. I didn't have what you'd call a special skill, and there weren't many instances where my resourcefulness helped the company through difficult times. If I did anything wrong, it was that I'd aged passively without a fight. For some reason, the young employees, who spoke several languages, enjoyed life, and smoothly carried out their tasks, were like people who had seen enough of life. Their motto appeared to be to avoid conflict, ambition, and sticky familial relationships. Because of these young people, I felt alienated at work. My social life wasn't faring better. Most of the text messages I received were updates from the elementary school where my oldest child had just started. I needed a change.

One day, as I was drafting a proposal for a new project, my husband came into the office with a carton of juice. It wasn't a special day when you gave chocolates or candy to your lover, and I hadn't taken the car when he'd needed it. I couldn't remember the last time he'd dropped by. It was the strangest thing.

"Why'd you bring such a small carton? Just look at how many people there are."

While I fussed, he leaned back in my chair and spun himself around. "I didn't know your company was so nice." He left soon after, but I found a post-it stuck in a bankbook that had a loan of 30 million won. It read: "I'm really sorry, but can you please pay this off?"

There wasn't much work to do, so I went to go see my husband's best friend K, the apparel company CEO my husband had lent money to. Apparently, he'd played the piano well since he was a boy, and thanks to his parents, he'd had a refined musical education and knew the names of most classical pieces. I discovered this refined friend eating black bean noodles for lunch or dinner, who knows, in the lobby of an unfurnished office building in Yeongdeungpo. The chili pepper shaker and dish of pickled radish were on the floor, and behind the men were stacks of cardboard boxes.

Not knowing how to bring up the money he owed, I bit my trembling lips and waited outside the building until the men were finished eating. Soon after, K came outside, holding a pack of cigarettes, and I greeted him awkwardly. He seemed bewildered to see me, for his face stiffened right away. I couldn't exactly grab him by the collar or get a written statement from him. I also wasn't there to make small talk and ask how long he'd played the piano. But he spoke first. "Please, don't tell my wife."

This is the kind of thing people said after making a mess.

The next afternoon, I called K's wife and lied to her, saying, "I happen to be in the area," and barged into her home. Her two boys were running around the house, and she was swigging beer in broad daylight, with a pile of empty bottles beside her. The boys took the ice cream I'd brought and went into their room. She was composed.

"We lost everything. We had to pull the kids from their afterschool programs. Look at them, all they do is play."

I needed some courage to say what I'd come to say, so I had a glass of beer as well. Just as I was wiping my lips to speak, she said, "Do you buy clothes? Who buys clothes these days anyway? Do you? If no one's buying women's clothes, who'll buy men's clothes? That's why we couldn't help going out of business."

Judging by the gouge in the center of the wardrobe and all the chipped and broken furniture in the apartment, they seemed to have been fighting a lot.

"Yeah, I still buy clothes." This is what I said as consolation. Or had she baited me?

Becoming more agitated, she jiggled her thighs that were exposed below her shorts. "Then things aren't that tough for you. We had to cancel our kids' insurance plans. Everything that man has is garbage. Everything inside those boxes—it's not even worth 500 won each. He drags them here and there, because he can't sell them, and then they get beat up and damaged. They're all garbage."

Were we actually better off? I'd gone there to get my money back, but I ended up giving the kids some allowance.

It was the wife of A, another friend of my husband's, who told me that K had separated from his wife and now slept at his office, using folded up boxes as blankets. It turned out A had lent B some money as well, and C had underwritten D's debt. These men had paired off and entered into a transaction that they'd kept a secret from their wives as well as their other friends. Based on the information I obtained from various sources, I organized all their business dealings into a chart, and presented it to my husband. Amazed, he asked how I'd managed to catch on to a situation he hadn't fully understood. Since he knew he'd made a mistake, he didn't come near me at bedtime and agreed with everything I said, so there was no need for us to fight. Because of our growing personal debt, plus his friend's debt we'd taken on, my speech and manners grew harsher and I no longer feared anything. Money seemed like a joke, and I had ludicrous dreams, like leading an excavation team at a giant oil field or hitting the jackpot.

Then one day, the wife of the former gas station owner invited everyone for dinner, and regardless of how much we seethed with anger, we got dressed up and went to relieve some stress. The smell of food and warmth should have greeted us when the front door opened, but we felt a chill as we walked through the entrance that was twice as long as most apartments. We gathered around the sofa and noticed we were all wearing dark clothes, and even the children playing in the next room were unusually quiet. The gas station owner's wife was a tall, beautiful woman who had studied in the United States, but her face was pinched and drawn, and she looked plain, like an ordinary woman.

"The reason I asked all of you to come today—"

Right then, her husband, who was sitting next to her, sat up and yelled, "I told you to shut up!"

"You see? This is the kind of treatment I get. I don't care about not having money. But being treated like this—I just can't take it anymore. I can't try throw away my pride."

"Don't be like that!" we said to her husband, rushing to her defense. "Why are you treating her this way?"

Now that she'd won our sympathy, the expression on her face changed. "Thank you. But the reason I asked you to come today is because of the money your husbands borrowed from my husband."

It turned out, these high school friends hadn't merely paired off like K and my husband to lend and borrow money. As the situation grew worse, they had changed partners and done the same thing. Then what did this have to do with the gas station owner? Before they had changed partners—so in other words, in the very beginning, before any of that happened—he had lent money to each person, at least once. He'd been a good friend.

"Sure, we'll get a small inheritance from our parents eventually, but how can friends rip us off like this? We don't know when we'll actually get our inheritance. We can't even pay the gas bill right now."

It turned out she was the one with the most accurate list of transactions. She handed out a photocopy of the list to each couple and told us to sign it after writing down the date we could pay back what we owed.

The men sat twirling their pencils, while the women merely gazed at the men's fingers. The mood was truly bizarre. A boy came out from the children's room and yelled, "Mom, we want pizza!" but the adults ignored him. Another boy came out and yelled, "Mom, we went some fried chicken!" but no one said anything.

"Why don't we talk about this later? The kids seem hungry. Should we go eat somewhere?" When one of the men finally spoke up, everyone stood to check their phones and use the bathroom, attempting to change the mood.

"Who said you could get up without signing? Please sit down," the gas station owner's wife said, pointing at the men.

"Hey, why should we have to clean up the mess the men made?" one woman cried, undoing her scarf from around her neck.

"How could you? How dare you say that to me right now?"

Everyone was getting worked up. "All right, all right, we understand how you feel. We really do. So why don't we eat first and talk?"

That day, for the first time in my life, I saw a gun. The gas station owner glared at us, holding a gun to his head. "Everyone, shut up this instant! You look down on me now because my business failed, don't you?"

Who would keep talking after that? We didn't move. We had to stay calm. The second his face crumpled, I squeezed my eyes shut. It seemed I heard the gun go off. Right then, we heard a girl's voice.

"Honey, did you check the stock market this morning? Why didn't you check it?"

The children were playing house in the next room. Everyone snickered soon after, and luckily nothing happened that day.

To be honest, what I said about having dated only three men was a lie. But I considered my husband to be my third and last man. However, that very night following the incident with the gun, he disappeared from this world. Not just him, but the other five men who had been at the house as well. The wives started calling one another to look for their husbands. I contacted the nearest police station right away. The police said they'd never had a case where a group of men went missing at the same time and were sold off to go work on a ship. "Maybe they went fishing?" they said.

We believed our men would return soon, so we even made bets with one another on when they would return. Until then, we truly believed they were holed up somewhere, drinking to their hearts' content to cope with the stress.

Whenever we had spare time, we went to the bars or BBQ restaurants our men had frequented, and sat among the other customers and drank soju. Men, who were dressed exactly like our men, sat drinking beer and soju, shaking their heads with laughter. After going from bar to bar, we'd get drunk and head home. Once home, I'd find my husband standing in front of the stove in his pajamas, nonchalantly boiling some instant noodle, or sleeping on the sofa, with a newspaper over his face.

A month went by, but the men didn't come back. One of the wives said they'd probably bought a small remote island with the money they'd skimmed and were now having the time of their lives. When a travel brochure about Greenland, the northernmost island on earth, was discovered in one of their bags, we assumed the men had gone there. Traveling by dogsled, surrounded by the dancing beautiful lights of the aurora borealis . . . It seemed plausible they were there. After all, the people of Greenland are known to be good at keeping secrets. They would ask no questions.

I even visited the restaurant where the men had been shooting their own Hong Kong noir. The mirror was broken once again, but this time, the main characters were college students in skinny jeans. The owner with the potty mouth bit her lips and the floor glittered with broken glass. At the emergency room, the girl who'd been constipated was still constipated, and she was waiting in the early hours before dawn to get an enema. She fiddled with her cell phone. While her mother went to settle the hospital bill, the girl called her friend and said, "I think the doctor touched my ass when he was giving me an enema."

When I'd finally come home after wandering around the city, my husband and the kids would be horsing around. They'd stand in the entrance and let out a fart and keel over with laughter. Months went by, but the men did not come home.

Then one day, the wives and I went to the last remaining place—the "pole" club they headed to when they were in a great mood. We'd each searched our homes to find old credit card statements and business cards and finally managed to find the room salon they had visited. However, we were denied entry. A brawny man in a suit came out and said, "This is not the kind of place for women to drink and talk." It didn't matter if people took us to be idiots who thought room salons were where you drank coffee and talked. We needed to go inside. On the second day, we told them the truth, but it was no use. They didn't budge. "If there's a problem, why don't you take it up with the police?"

The winter was colder than usual. The kids grew, regardless of whether their dad was around or not, and I somehow managed to not get fired. As always, the responsibility of overseeing projects went to younger, smarter colleagues, while I took on the job of assisting them, since I knew the kind of things they would miss. Working at the same company for a long time was certainly an asset, but I'd probably last another year or two at the most. Though no one was telling me to quit right now.

One weekend afternoon, I was waiting at a streetlight on my way home from the store when I saw a promotional bus for a nightclub stopped at the crosswalk. On the side of the bus was a picture of men in sunglasses and white T-shirts, but their faces looked so familiar I nearly dropped my phone.

It was them. Their physique and hair styles had changed, but there was no doubt about it. It made me jealous to see them having a grand old time. As soon as the light changed, the bus took off. Watching it pull away, I hit my chest. Where could they be?

On the following weekend, the kids dashed to the playground first thing in the morning, before even eating breakfast. "Mom! Dad! It snowed!" The voices of children rang out through the complex. I stopped making breakfast and followed my kids out. It had snowed a lot during the night. My feet sank into the snow and the tip of my nose stung from the chill. My children romped around clearing paths, building snowmen, hardly noticing their gloves were sopping wet. My oldest said she was going to build a daddy snowman, and my youngest said she was going to build a mommy snowman. They came inside to get a necktie and hat and decorated the daddy snowman, while the only thing the mommy snowman got was a scarf. The harsh weather continued into the afternoon and the children played in the snow, sweating.

The next morning, I went to take out the recycling and saw that the daddy snowman wasn't there. Of course, the mommy snowman next to it was also gone. Both had melted away in the strong morning light, and only a necktie and hat remained where the daddy snowman had been.

City of Anxiety

WHEN HE RECEIVED the call telling him she had left home, he was at a karaoke bar in Daehak-ro. He'd been there for several hours after a round of drinks with colleagues, though all he could think about was the proposal he needed to write up and present in the morning. As soon as he heard the voice of the woman he still called Mother, he sat up straight and glanced at those sitting next to him. Her frail, worried voice—as she asked if they happened to be together or when they'd last talked, and then apologized for these questions—sounded the same from several years ago. All he could do was to tell her not worry. Most likely, her friends had loaded her in a car and dragged her off to the coast, or she was crashing at a friend's house, yakking the night away. As he sat there in a daze, the beer that someone sprayed toward the ceiling fell on his face, catching him by surprise, and he ended up biting the inside of his right cheek. The room erupted as people sprayed beer at a colleague celebrating his birthday. People laughed and cried. He didn't think much of the phone call, aside from feeling a little bad for not asking after the old woman's health or how she was doing, and for not answering the phone more gently. He said goodbye to his colleagues, and they each climbed into a cab. As soon as he got home, he brushed his teeth and crawled into bed.

The weekend came and the weather was mild with little yellow dust. It was a rare weekend that he didn't have to work, and he wanted a proper rest. Until this point, he hardly thought about the woman. He didn't want to jump to conclusions. After sleeping to his heart's content on Saturday and again on Sunday, he went for a light jog at the park across from his apartment and then headed to the bathhouse. He changed into the terracotta-colored clothes they gave him and lay down in the hot stone room where heated tiles were spread out on the floor. A few people wearing the Princess Leia towel-do walked in and whispered with one another. The more work there was to do, the more people he had to meet, and the more he had to go to the bathhouse. By Thursday afternoon, his body was so stiff he could hardly move. It was a vicious cycle. If he felt better, he overdid it, and then he'd have to go to the bathhouse to loosen up. The tiles grew hotter. He dozed off, and the whispering turned to laughter for a moment. His head spun and his vision grew blurry, so he slowly sat up. His whole body was soaked with sweat. For the first time, he began to worry that something had happened to her. He retrieved his cell phone from the locker and called her house. Her mother answered in the same voice and said she still hadn't heard anything.

A week later on the following Sunday, he found himself wearing the bathhouse clothes once more, sweating in the hot stone room. As if something suddenly occurred to him, he got to his feet and hurried into the changing room. He took off his clothes, showered, and headed outside. He thought of many things while on his way to Ogin-dong. Her home was unchanged from several years before. The old woman, probably about seventy-five years old by now, was lying down watching television, with her head propped on a white pillow. The younger brother, whose name or age he could no longer recall, was the one who answered the door. "Is it your sister?" the old woman called out, sitting up. She tried to say something else, but her voice didn't seem to be working.

The three sat without speaking, like small, isolated islands. Shortly after, the brother went into her room and returned with her old cell phone. It was the same one she used when they had lived together.

"I don't think she talked to anyone recently. The only thing I could find in her call history is when she talked to you several months ago."

Her mother's face crumpled. He couldn't tell if she was crying or smiling. In some ways, it looked like she was smiling. "Where could she be?" she asked. A few seconds later, her face contorted into an expression of pain.

He didn't know what to say. "I'll try looking for her. You've got to keep up your strength. I'm sure she's fine, so please try not to worry."

He'd stopped by the Paris Croissant at the major intersection in front of the building. He nudged the cake toward the old woman and got to his feet. He considered looking into the woman's room, but didn't. He looked back from the entrance and saw the old woman silently stroking the top of the cake box.

He walked slowly along the dark Ogin-dong alley. It was just as dim as when he'd first walked the woman home so many years ago. It was April, but still very chilly, and the sky that was hazy with fog or yellow dust grazed his head. All of a sudden, the click-clack of her heels rang out, just like long ago when they'd walked down the alley together. Not that she'd worn high heels often, as he could only recall her being in running shoes after they grew close. If she did wear dress shoes, she opted for plain flats with no decoration. He walked slowly past a cosmetics shop, behind a couple pushing a stroller, and then past a darkened studio. *One day I want to write about this neighborhood*, she used to say once they were married, on their way home after visiting her family in Ogin-dong. These words seemed to swoop out of the alley and stick to his back. The street led to a market. He took in the stony faces of the vendors cleaning their stalls. He walked past large bowls brimming with clams and fish, a fruit stand, a shoe repair shop, a tailor shop, all the way to the butcher shop at the main entrance of the market. He looked back. He was stunned by the warmth that seemed to be coming alive under his arm and along his side, the same sensation he'd felt whenever he put his arm around her shoulders. He stood glued to the spot, as if he'd swallowed one of the hot tiles from the bathhouse.

Once home, he copied all the messages and phone numbers on her cell phone into a notebook. Though he was hungry, he didn't feel like cooking, and he didn't want to go to a crowded restaurant by himself. He wrote out promotional texts, like "Loans up to 10 million won available on same day—Happy Finance, Assistant Manager Kim," and messages from people he couldn't recall the faces of, as well as all the phone numbers in her contacts. He told himself everything would be fine, as long as he got in touch with her before leaving on his business trip in three weeks. He was sure she'd gone on a spontaneous road trip or she was holed up at a friend's house, watching DVDs, not caring that her family might be worried sick.

"She just walked out. She didn't even get changed. I don't know what she was wearing because she just left. I can't even remember if she was wearing sweatpants or a long skirt."

Her younger brother, who'd followed him to the door of the building, had spoken in a flat, calm voice. In a burst of anger, he nearly asked why they hadn't filed a missing person report right away, why they hadn't cared for her more diligently, but he held back. These words were difficult for him to utter, since he himself had separated from her because he no longer wanted to live with her.

He didn't turn on the computer or the television. He didn't even feel like massaging his scalp with the expensive ampoules he'd purchased at the duty free on his way back from another business trip. He'd bought them to reverse the hair loss that had just begun. He felt sluggish. But he couldn't do anything, because he kept seeing in his mind the woman walking out onto the main street in Ogin-dong with her hands jammed in her sweater pockets. Sometimes it was her left foot that first popped out of the alley, sometimes her torso, and sometimes he heard her voice first.

It started raining on Monday morning. He worked all morning without taking a break, checking everything meticulously, then left the office and got into a cab. He went to see K, who had been her closest friend. K lived on the 24th floor of an apartment building in Mapo and was busy looking after her baby, who was crawling around on the floor. The apartment was cluttered, with two large drying racks in the living room, and piles of toys, diapers, household items, and garbage everywhere. Whenever he tried to ask her a serious question, the baby would fall on her bottom or put something in her mouth, take it out, and start to wail. His colleague called, asking where he'd disappeared to at lunchtime, but the call was dropped for some reason. He couldn't tell if it was raining outside, and he couldn't hear the rain either. While K stood at the table, preparing some instant coffee, the baby scurried toward a cloth book by the open balcony door. He glanced out the window at the gray sky and picked up the baby around the waist, setting her back down in the living room away from the balcony. The baby had felt doughy, like a rubber doll, and alien, too.

"The connection isn't good here, because we're so high up. I haven't seen that girl for ages. I think I only saw her a few times after you two got married. You haven't changed at all. Men don't really change, but women get old."

As K raised her arms to tie her long hair, he caught a whiff of something fishy. He couldn't tell if it was sweat or breastmilk, but he found the smell extremely off-putting, and he wanted to leave the apartment as soon as possible.

When the elevator reached the ground floor, even before he could step out, some middle-aged women with expressionless faces walked in, turned, and stared at the door. The apartment lacked a proper lobby and started from the second floor, since it was built on pilotis. The space under the structure seemed more like an austere factory or government building, with the columns and colorful recycling bins lined up against the concrete wall as the only decorations.

oh no, what should I do? I don't know who else to ask

When he received K's text, which she seemed to have sent in a hurry, he was staring at the dingy low-rises huddled next to the apartment building. He left the complex and climbed into a taxi.

• • •

Two days later, he met J, another one of her friends. A helper in the kitchen at a ramen shop near Hongdae, J wasn't a friend who suited the woman, who'd been introverted and shy. She was wearing a black kerchief wrapped around her head, an apron, and yellow rubber gloves. As soon as she stepped out of the kitchen, she took off her dirty gloves that were covered with mushy noodles. Her hands were dark pink and seemed to be burning up. J wasn't able to tell him anything about the woman either.

"We've been so busy we lost touch. Please come in. At least have a bowl of ramen before you go."

With a smile, he handed her his business card and said he would contact her. The second J pushed aside the blue Japanese-style curtain and went back into the kitchen, a voice bawled loudly in Japanese as if he'd been waiting. He walked down to the Hongdae station entrance, jostled by the crowds, and overcome by hunger, stepped into a fast-food joint. After skimming the menu, he ordered a ramen and gazed outside. He ate, thinking that even if he managed to find her, he'd better prepare himself for the fact that she'd look different. After all, he'd seen her for the last time three years ago.

Whenever he found a spare minute at work, he called the numbers he'd copied from the list of contacts in her cell phone. Some numbers were no longer in service. When he'd cross off a number, one by one, it would already be lunchtime, and he would surge out onto the street with his colleagues, as if nothing were the matter. It was spring, and the women walking on the streets were in slingbacks, and he also noticed their skirts were shorter, too. The streets were full of office workers wearing company ID badges around their necks, and the day threatened to turn hot at any moment. But at night, it turned chilly. On those nights, he pressed the speed dial button for his own number on her cell phone. As if someone were calling him, he would then stare down at the phone in his hand for a long time. The name Mina on his display screen seemed to him like some mysterious sign.

His business trip was approaching. Due to the nature of the assignment, he couldn't send someone else instead. There was no way around it—he had to go himself. He stopped going to the bathhouse, and he also stopped going for jogs. His face turned sallow, to the extent he didn't even want to look in the mirror, and his hair fell out in clumps into the sink. He wasn't taking any supplements and he wasn't eating much, but his belly still stuck out, and he became tired as soon as he ate. The pile of clothes he needed to take to the drycleaner only grew bigger, and the laundry room and bathroom needed a good cleaning. He headed home right after work, but any plans to tackle some household chores vanished as soon as he walked through the front door. He didn't want to lift a finger. In just a week or two, his routine had been disturbed, and though he was aware of it, there was nothing he could do. He'd fantasize about pushing his penis into a woman's crotch, his penis that stayed flaccid no matter how erotic his fantasies were, and then fall asleep.

He went to the old apartment outside of Seoul where they had lived together after getting married. Not because he thought she'd be there, but because there was nothing he could do. He told himself he had no choice but to go, because if she still wasn't back after he'd returned from his two-week business trip, he sensed his life would become extremely difficult.

When they lived there, they had commuted to their jobs in Seoul. They eventually got rid of their small car, but she'd called it their son. He did most of the driving, while she picked up things to eat in the car after work, like gimbap, soondae sausages, and sandwiches, since they got home late due to the traffic and were too hungry to start making dinner then. If there was a problem on a military base or facility in northern Gyeonggi Province, or a festival was taking place, the roads would come to a standstill for an hour, sometimes two. As soon as they got in the car, they complained about their bosses or co-workers for about half an hour. But if they ran into bad traffic, one would ask who loved who more, and this sometimes developed into a fight. If they happened to see fireworks from the 88 Expressway, they laughed and kissed each other deeply, not caring if the people in other cars saw. Sometimes they'd get stirred up and stick a finger inside a shirt or under a skirt and pass the time that way. Back then, he'd never thought time could go by so quickly, that there would be a time when he'd helplessly grow old like this.

He looked around for a long time. There was no trace of the old five-story buildings that had lined the street. The landscape was the same, but their old building was gone and the road was also a lot wider than before. He sat at the bus stop across the street with his chin in his hand, gazing straight ahead and in the direction the bus would come from, as if waiting for someone. Yes, their low-rise had been there. The proof was in the hideous high-voltage lines and utility poles that still ran along the street. He drew a square in the air with his finger and marked a dot in one spot. Dusty buses came speeding down the street and children wearing backpacks walked by, eating ice cream. It grew dark in no time. After a while, he got up and crossed the street. He wandered along the street, as if he had some business at the new apartment construction site, even fiddling with the hard hats that were hanging on a rack. The workers in hard hats, standing atop the unfinished tower, looked as small as ants.

Several dump trucks were transporting construction materials, panting like exhausted dogs. He tried to estimate where his apartment had been, but it was hard to tell. He guessed it was somewhere between the new tower and new sidewalk. His building was long gone.

Before he left for his business trip, there was a department dinner. Everyone seemed overly sensitive that night, but as always, something ridiculous became the problem. One called another by the wrong title, beer bottles were knocked down and set rolling on the floor, and the female staff ran out of the restaurant, screaming. Putting pressure on the torn corner of his mouth with his palm, he pulled out his wallet and paid. He'd been the one to throw the first punch, but a fist had come back in turn, and he'd knocked down his colleague with another punch. This colleague was now trying to fight off the others, who had him by the arm on each side and were dragging him out of the restaurant. His whole department, including the female staff who'd fled, was nowhere to be seen. He crouched down in front of the darkened window of a department store. His lip had stopped bleeding, but his eye was swelling up. He unzipped the pocket of his bag and fished out the woman's phone. He pressed a few buttons and opened her photo album. Magnolia blooms one would see anywhere in springtime filled the screen. He went through the whole album, but there wasn't a single selfie, not even a black screen because she'd snapped a picture by mistake.

Two days later, he received a call from Ogin-dong. Her brother said he'd filed a missing person report with the police but that there wasn't much they could do about a simple disappearance. When he asked how their mother was doing, the brother replied, "So-so. She's getting by."

He scrolled through his list of contacts to see if he knew anyone with connections to the police, but not a single person worked in the legal field.

He saw Y. After dinner and coffee, they checked into the small hotel they usually went to. He opened the present from Y—a necktie. "Wear it on your business trip," she said.

He liked perhaps half of everything about her, and disliked the other half, but didn't want to show it. No arguments or interrogations or fights—that was his creed.

"Why do you look so tired? Do you want to hear a funny story?" she asked.

Come to think of it, she was a legal administrative assistant. He laughed to himself, imagining telling her about the woman. Y didn't show it, but he knew he hadn't pleased her in bed. He was probably the reason why an air of awkwardness lingered between them after sex. He grinned again, thinking about a penis enlargement surgery, as if grateful for the existence of this procedure, which could save men with certain shortcomings. He told himself it was a good thing he could still hold onto hope, despite his many problems.

The next evening, he went to watch a movie by himself. The theater located on the fourth floor of the old building near Insadong was a place she had loved.

It's incredible that a building like this still exists, don't you think? In my opinion, the architect who designed this building is the best, though he died too early. But whoever designs a building like this has to die early, since he must have thought really hard. It was probably hard on him. There's nothing more difficult than wrestling with ideas.

The theater on the fourth floor was connected to the next building. The connecting passageway and roof terrace served as an outdoor lounge for cinema goers and the exit was through the next building. Her voice rang across the terrace, as if it were coming through speakers. He stood listening, bewildered.

You don't know anything about architecture or films, do you? People who don't know those things are unhappy.

Her mocking voice seemed to be coming from somewhere on the terrace. He stood among the young people in colorful clothes who had come to watch a flick and looked out at the view while sipping his coffee. He'd had no idea that they were screening a film for free that day and that it was a Japanese film. He'd merely stood in line behind the others and followed the person in front of him into the theater. There were no commercials or previews, just a single picture of an emergency evacuation map, and the film started immediately. He fell asleep right away. It was the first time in a long while that he'd been able to sleep so well. The black-and-white movie was about destitute poverty. Maybe because he had slept through the first half of the movie, but the second half was dull. He simply managed to recall having wanted to learn Japanese if he ever had the opportunity. When he stepped outside at the end of the movie, the air had grown cold. He leaned against the terrace railing and gazed down at the street where cars sped by and watched the young people smoke, their long hair blowing in the wind. Half of the terrace was lit up, while the other half was dark, within the shadow cast by the next building. It was then that he saw her.

She stood in the middle of the terrace, a white canvas bag slung over her shoulder as always. People who came out from the theater hurried down the stairs, followed by those who had been smoking in the corner. However, she didn't budge. She continued to stand in the middle of the concrete terrace.

That's it, I got you now.

In his excitement, he lost his balance as he rose from the bench and stumbled. All of a sudden, she turned and dashed toward the stairs. He hurried after her, rushing from the fourth floor down to the first floor, but she was gone. Instead, pig heads displayed in front of soondae restaurants kept watch over the night street. He set out without thinking, dragging himself along, so bloated with exhaustion that he felt like he was going to burst. He didn't bother getting on a bus or subway and walked all the way home.

The next day, he received an email from the factory he was supposed to visit in China. They asked if he could postpone the trip by a week. The news was neither bad nor good. He updated his superiors about the change and was compensated accordingly. Though the trip was just a formality, it was still necessary. He thought about the snow that would be everywhere, about taking a sleeper train through northeast China for seventeen hours. He felt exhausted just thinking about it. If he was lucky, he might be able to see thick white snow falling outside his window. Chinese instant cup noodles tasted pretty good and if he took naps, seventeen hours would pass by soon enough. The landscape, not yet touched by urbanization, somewhat comforted him. While he was thinking about the landscape he'd see on the way to the factory, he received a call from the woman's friend K, who lived in Mapo. "I was wondering if you had any news." He could hear the baby wailing beside her.

"I'm sure she's fine. By the way, make sure you keep the balcony door closed. The rails seemed a bit wide. It looked dangerous." While he overstepped his bounds and said these things, the call was dropped. A few seconds later, he received a text from K.

I can see why Mina liked you I hope you can find her soon she's such a sweet girl

After lunch, he picked up a coffee and was heading back to the office when he received a call from the Ogin-dong house.

"I'm sorry, but I was wondering if you could go. Mom was the one who received the call from the police. I told her not to worry, that we still need to check, but she's been shaking all day and won't eat a thing. To be honest, I'm more worried about Mom. I feel so bad for her. I should stay with her."

After he hung up, he realized he was shaking.

"Do you know this woman?"

The police officer showed him a few pictures. He flipped through the photos quickly.

"No, this isn't her. I don't know this person."

The officer asked him about his relationship to the missing person, and he grew so upset that he wanted to bolt out of the station. He hated the officer's tone. He hated the brutality of someone judging his life without knowing anything, of having the gall to talk about it so casually.

"Ah jeez, maybe it's time you stopped worrying about your ex and moved on," the officer said.

He couldn't erase the woman in the photos from his mind. It wasn't her features that were important but the circumstance. He went into a coffee shop on a darkening side street in Seochon. When they were dating, even up until they were married, Seochon was a quiet, underdeveloped neighborhood near the Blue House. However, it was now a trendy place full of posh restaurants and antique furniture shops. He drank two cups of coffee and took in the neighborhood's transformation. But the changes failed to hold his attention for long. The woman in the pictures had been discovered in the shadowy back of a park, her body badly decomposed because she'd been dead for a long time. Most likely a suicide. He hoped the woman wouldn't resort to that. He believed that no one should inflict such damage on themselves. He pulled out his phone and found her number and dialed. A phone vibrated inside his bag. He grew angrier. With his phone clenched in his hand, he began to rant.

"Quit fooling around! I have to go on a business trip. We didn't come all this way just for us to turn out this way. It's my fault, okay? It's all my fault."

For one whole week, he roamed about the city instead of heading home after work. He stood in front of a fish stall at the Ogin-dong market and stared blankly at the mudfish swimming inside the rubber barrel. Though there was no one to eat it, he bought rice cakes and strawberries packed in Styrofoam containers. He walked into a Seochon book café and browsed the titles of books from one end of the store to the other. He sometimes walked through Samcheong-dong to the Bugak Skyway Promenade, or made his way down a Buam-dong alley, all the way to Gugi-dong. The paths they had walked together were gone without a trace, or completely rebuilt, or in the process of changing. He told himself that only weak and stupid humans didn't change. If he stepped into a shop or restaurant, he became the last customer to leave, and he often left his umbrella or cell phone behind. He roamed about the city, like someone who had lost their mind. He felt his body dry up and his eyes grow dim. If he happened to see his reflection in a full-length mirror in a large lobby, he became incredibly flustered. The person walking toward the mirror was a perfect stranger.

One night he was walking past the bus stop in front of the Seoul Museum of History toward the Salvation Army building. The wind blew so hard even walking was difficult, and the yellow dust had turned the air murky and gray. Right then, he saw her push open the door of an old coffee shop on the corner of the street and walk inside. It was her. Without thinking, he charged straight for the shop and bounced off the glass. The staff ran out of the shop in shock and a customer who'd been about to push the door open to leave was so flustered they didn't know what to do. Blood flowed down his face. The metal frame of his glasses had broken and cut a deep gash into his temple. The bridge had also cracked, but more importantly, he couldn't see anything. He pressed the towel the coffee shop worker handed him against his eye and waited for the ambulance to come. It arrived almost immediately, and before he had the chance to thank the staff, he was transported to Kangbuk Samsung Hospital, which was the nearest hospital. A doctor dressed in a blue surgical gown asked him how he'd gotten injured, in detail, just as the police officer had. The gash stung and the smell of disinfectant was overpowering.

"We need to know what happened in order to treat it. We need to understand how serious the injury is. Thank goodness nothing went in your eye. You're lucky. Or should I say unlucky?"

• • •

He saw her again at the Cheonggye Stream near Gwanghwamun Sinmunno. She sat huddled over on one of the steps leading down to the stream, dressed in a checkered coat she liked to wear in the spring and fall. At first he doubted his eyes, but it was definitely her. It was an April night when yellow dust was at its peak. She looked exhausted, but she was as playful as ever. She took off her shoes and shook them in front of her face, and she blocked her ears, shouting, "Ahh! Ahh!" Keeping his eyes on her, he approached her slowly. Cars that were being diverted from Gwanghwamun Square ignored the detour sign and rushed toward him, but he didn't move out of the way. He clasped the iron railing of a bridge-like installation piece and was about to call out to her when she stood up and started walking. He followed her. She plodded to the crosswalk in front of the old news building, which was now being used as an art gallery. Volunteers campaigning in the late hours shouted at the top of their lungs. She continued to trudge on. He arrived at the crosswalk, and standing behind several people, gazed down at the woman's shoulder. The light changed and she started crossing the street very slowly. The people behind her went ahead until she and he were the only ones still crossing the street. She rounded the Kyobo Bookstore building. The U.S. embassy guards strolled back and forth in front of the bus stop. As soon as she reached the crosswalk leading to Gwanghwamun Square, she sank down onto the sidewalk. Her hair looked a lot longer and she had grown thinner. She looked as if she'd aged ten, twenty years. She bent over and stared at the concrete ground without looking up. All her movements, as she reached for something or turned her head, seemed sluggish and powerless. He could tell it had nothing to do with growing old. It had to do with passion. She seemed to have lost it all. The light changed and she trudged toward the square once more. The only people in the square seemed to be tourists with cameras and couples on dates. He followed her. Every time she took a step, he heard a stomp and the ground shook a little. A camera flashed. He heard laughter and a foreign language he couldn't place. He looked around, as if he were seeing the square for the first time. Dazzling billboards filled the sky, and on one side, he saw the night sky above the old palace and newly built statue of King Sejong. When the signal changed, people crossed, and when it didn't, people stopped. There was noticeably less traffic, and in just a few steps, he'd be able to catch up to her.

"Stop! Stop right there!" he shouted, but she kept walking.

Every time she moved, the sound of heavy footsteps rang out, and a foul smell spread across the square. He reached out to grasp her shoulder. At that instant, her shoulder crumbled under his hand. The lights shining down on the concrete grew brighter and people hurried out of the square and crossed the street.

"Talk to me! What are you doing, wandering around like this?" he shouted, but she walked faster. The square sloped down toward Gwanghwamun station. She plodded along. People handing out flyers thrust a piece of paper toward her. As soon as she took it, she tossed it into the air, and strangely enough, it landed on his face. He peeled it off his glasses, but when he looked ahead again, she was gone. It had happened in an instant. He glanced around. All he could see was concrete, lit up by the white lights. The anxious city. He gazed blankly at the digital billboard flashing in the distance, wondering where he was supposed to look for her now.

Pripyat Storage

IN 2006, I WAS THIRTY YEARS OLD. Like any other year, there were 365 days in 2006, though spring and fall were unusually short. Nothing happened. I seemed to have shrunk a little and my hair started thinning at the crown, but I wasn't diagnosed with a serious illness. That in itself was a blessing.

April 26, 2006, marked the twenty-year-anniversary of the Chernobyl disaster. It was an event I commemorated, though no one else did.

Did anyone else see the acid rain, which fell all morning downtown? Or the yellow dust that covered the murky night sky when the rain finally stopped? I believed it was a message from Chernobyl. Perhaps the radiation released into the air following the disaster had arrived in Seoul just then.

That day, members of a particular religious group were stationed on the overpass, tapping the shoulders of those passing by, warning them of the end times. In the downtown shopping district, cats and pigeons attacked the garbage bags left out in front of restaurants, scattering the contents all over the sidewalk, and the manhole cover on the street shuddered constantly, as if something were about to spew out. Strangely enough, everything I put in my mouth kept getting stuck in my throat, so I ate nothing the whole day. I pulled back the lace curtain over the small kitchen sink window and watched the dark sky all night. Neither the apartment nor the mountains collapsed, but I was positive I had received a message from Chernobyl. Why else would my entire body be damp? It had to be evidence of radiation. It wasn't a dream.

Actually, there was one important thing that took place. It happened on a certain day in September, shortly after the anniversary of my father's death. After a nice lunch, my mother and I returned to the office, and as usual, she asked me to make her some instant coffee. I mixed two cups of coffee the same way I always did and placed them on the coffee table, sitting on the sofa across from her. It was then that she pushed a piece of paper toward me.

I, Kim Yeongchul (60 years old this year), give Best Storage to my daughter.

I burst into laughter. Putting her age in parentheses was a bit funny. This Kim Yeongchul had spent her whole life working at Best Storage. I was more used to seeing her in the warehouse office than in the kitchen at home. She would sit glued to her desk and devote herself to balancing the books. She always used the same model of pencil and eraser, and her handwriting hadn't changed over the years. Even her electronic calculator resembled her. She set mouse traps in every corner of the warehouse and cheerfully disposed of the mice. She was a truly odd person, whose incredible memory enabled her to remember every tenant she ever met. However, there was no sign of regret on her face over this decision. How could she simply hand over the warehouse to me? I hadn't expected this at all. I signed the paper without thinking and put it in the plastic folder where we kept all the important business documents.

The next day, Kim Yeongchul outfitted herself in luxurious hiking gear and set out for the mountains. I had no idea when she'd made such preparations. For someone like me, who detested both the mountains and the sea, I lacked the skills to even picture where she was headed. Why would she put herself through so much trouble to climb a mountain that would stay in the same spot year after year? Those were the limits of my imagination. When I called to ask about the warehouse or other matters, she didn't answer. If I finally managed to get through, she said the same thing, to do as I wished, whatever seemed reasonable, since I was the boss. All she did was give me the usual spiel. How could she be so callous?

The first order of business was to change the warehouse name. I thought about calling it *H Storage* or *C Storage*, but I didn't like either of them. However, I also didn't want to inherit the name *Best Storage*, which we had used back when my father was still alive. My mother had kept the same name all this time. That's when I thought of *Pri Storage*.

Pripyat is the name of a city near Chernobyl where the nuclear power plant had been located. I don't know if this is right, but it used to be a closed city when Ukraine was a part of the Soviet Union, so top secret that it couldn't even be found on a map. A city with only apartment complexes to house the people needed to run the power plant. Nobody could have guessed I'd gotten the storage name by taking the first syllable of a city that had become a ghost town after the nuclear accident. No matter what anyone said, I came from Pripyat. Pripyat was my true home.

I don't know when or who first started to say this, but friends claimed that by the time we turned thirty, we'd all get cancer or some mystery illness, and kick the bucket. Maybe we arrived at this conclusion by taking the worst-case scenarios from countless European news programs forecasting the future—unverified words spewed by various media outlets to serve as a warning to rude, aimless young people.

It is predicted that in the next twenty years, UK residents will have the highest infertility rate, as well as the highest number of diseases. They are also likely to be the generation in history to face the highest unemployment rates.

Things that sounded as if they'd come straight out of baseless reports and supermarket tabloids started happening around me. A married friend kept miscarrying for unknown reasons, so much so that pregnancy became terror itself, and since she dreaded getting pregnant, she divorced her husband. Another friend was diagnosed with thyroid cancer and underwent chemotherapy, becoming so exhausted that she gave up all hope and could do nothing but stare at the wall. But the worst of all evils was unemployment. Nearly none of my friends had decent jobs. Everyone was unhappy, as if we'd all been destined for unhappiness.

I was the one who brought up the Chernobyl incident as proof that our generation would be the most unfortunate in human history. Like the children of Chernobyl, I expected to die of thyroid cancer, even though it would take another twenty, thirty years before we'd know the exact number of people who died from radiation exposure. This had happened all the way in Europe and there was no way the radiation had made its way to Seoul, so why did we believe we were the unluckiest generation in history?

"The wind must have carried it here. Or it could have oozed here underground. Slowly, little by little, for twenty years. Or birds could have carried it here on their bodies and spread it."

Friends blustered, drinking beer. I haven't checked to see if they continued to think this way after their twenties were over. However, I believed that some of us, like the children from Chernobyl, would end up with thyroid cancer and die a miserable death. If I didn't mentally prepare myself this way, my anxiety only grew, because I wouldn't be able to cope with the unhappiness heading my way. It was much better to think of myself as a potential cancer patient.

I've always been a Hwanghak-dong resident, back in 2006, around the time the restoration of the Cheonggye Stream was finished, and still today. Before the restoration, everything was so chaotic it was easy to get lost, but shops have been organized neatly into sections now. Even still, I lose my way more often. When I walk down the straight alleys that are no longer a maze, I find myself walking along the stream. Everything is clean and orderly, but the overall effect is rather flat. Hwanghak-dong's sky with its daytime moon looks dull and lifeless, like me as I grow older. Sometimes, the Hwanghak-dong sky faces the corner rooftop of the new high-rise building and looks as if it's about to burst. Maybe it's just me. Maybe I'm just jealous, since people grow old and get sick, but cities always transform into a new thing. Cities constantly change without ever having a chance to grow old. How lucky for them!

To guide people to Pri Storage, I wrote out detailed directions. I also drew multiple routes starting from the subway to make things easier for everyone.

Take Subway Line 2, get off at Sindang station, and use Exit 2. Once outside, you'll see Industrial Bank of

Korea. Face the entrance of IBK, turn left, and take a few steps until you come to Central Market. Central Market is a traditional outdoor market. Do not go in, but if you stand at the market entrance and look around, you'll see a yellow sign at about eye level with the words Sindang Creative Mall. Right below the sign, there is a side street. Walk down that side street and push open a small, strange glass door at the end and you'll see a long underground passage out of cobblestone.

There are many sashimi restaurants and eateries near the door. But keep walking along the underground passage and you'll see a long line of art studios. After you browse through the studios and walk to the end of the passage, you'll come to a security guard sitting at a desk. Greet him, turn to the left, and you'll see the last exit. It means you've walked below ground to the end of Central Market.

Once you go up the stairs and make your way past the exit, you'll see shops selling kitchenware. Turn left and that's Hwanghak-dong. However, Pri Storage isn't in Hwanghak-dong. We're on the other side of the road in the furniture district, directly in front of a playground. If you're not sure, look for people on sewing machines in the vacant lot in front of the playground. The white two-story building in front of the alterations shop is Pri Storage, the one with black lines streaking the outside. Welcome!

Whenever I opened the window, the stack of flyers I'd made but hadn't yet distributed dropped to the floor one page at a time. Because a high-rise building was going up right behind our warehouse, the noise of the excavator didn't stop all day long. The construction company had started digging as soon as they demolished the old building behind the warehouse. The noise was astounding. Sometimes it felt as though the excavator bucket would crash through the wall and scoop me up in my chair. There was a thin wall between the excavator and me at least, but the women who altered clothes outside my building didn't have even a single curtain or panel blocking them from the noise. Still, they seemed totally unfazed. Sometimes it made me angry to see them, the fact that they had to make a living this way. But regardless of the women, once the foundation was completed, the building grew taller each day. They said a state-of-the-art sauna was going in the basement of the 20-story building, so I guess it wasn't a bad thing if it meant all the overworked Hwanghak-dong women could go there to relax and raise their spirits. I picture the stone-faced women who'd been working at their sewing machines sitting in the hot, bubbling water. But look at the smiles spreading across their faces!

So how was Best Storage, the predecessor of Pri Storage, when it first opened? Before we moved here to the furniture district, our warehouse was around 200 square feet, maybe even smaller. A storage in name only, it was probably closer to a junk shop. The reason the business was able to expand was all thanks to my mother. It took her twenty years to go from a small junk shop to leasing an old building, growing it into a stable business. If that wasn't a miracle, what was? It was a great achievement. However, I had no confidence in bringing about a miracle like that.

When I returned to my parents' place after various failures in life, my father's health had deteriorated. The house was in total disarray. Sure, their apartment was in an old low-rise building, but despite their three bedrooms, they had no extra room. They simply had too much stuff. Since there wasn't a room I could use, I had no choice but to clean. I'd been cleaning for a few minutes when I started to feel sick. My father had filled the entire room with garbage. A plastic bag he'd filled with more plastic bags reeked of salted shrimp. After turning the bag upside down and pulling out all the bags, I found the offending container of salted shrimp, but it was no use. Paper bags that had been folded into small tiles kept pouring out from the side of the wardrobe and under the drawers. That wasn't all. I found dozens of stainless steel tubes of dubious purpose, a frying pan missing a handle, an old gas range with no connecting tube, and dozens of rusty old knives.

My father, who came back from the hospital, saw all the things I'd left outside the front door to discard. He frowned and grew very angry, and stood before the objects with his eyes closed, as if offering a prayer.

"I'm going to clean them up, so don't touch them!"

These things might as well have been garbage, but not to my father. He'd been holding onto them as valuables, but they were simply garbage. Though he was furious, he couldn't bring those things back into the house. He didn't have the strength. Looking at my father, who'd become worn out by collecting all this junk, I found the situation so ridiculous I could only laugh. How did other people's garbage become so important to him? In the end, he became garbage himself. No. He became a fistful of ashes.

After inheriting the business and stepping foot in the warehouse for the first time in a long while, I was a bit disappointed. I'd believed a cute little storage fairy lived there, but no, it was just a holding place for oversized junk. Pots and meal trays from a nearby kitchenware shop that had been kept there due to a lack of space were stacked up to the ceiling, and worn colorful velvet sofas that looked like stage props were piled on top of one another. Bundles of field jackets tied up with rope were hideous and when I opened a plastic box full of hundreds of the same doll, they all widened their eyes at me, saying, "Sis, please save us!"

Old musical instruments and shabby furniture, dozens of the same painting by an uncredited artist, and a box of crude glass cups—the collection of objects was truly eclectic. From antiques and broken clocks and brass junk to grimy vinyl records, obscure books, bizarre-looking electronic equipment, and big and small generators of unknowable purpose that resembled raccoons, they looked like garbage to me.

The first thing I did was to put up a notice asking everyone to pick up the items they had stored. I flipped through the ledgers crammed with my mom's handwritten entries and called every tenant. To my shock, she'd kept perfect books. She'd written in exact detail the number and condition of items even the owners themselves could no longer recall. Everything in the warehouse was tied with red rope, which was tagged with the item's dimensions and location. This perfectly matched the label stuck on the item itself, as well as the details recorded in the books.

"Just throw them out. That business went bust. Still, those were the days."

For those who answered this way, I felt bad, but I promptly lugged their things outside. Then the Hwanghak-dong Junk Man, who'd helped my mother through the years, loaded them onto his handcart and took them away. Was it true he'd bought himself a building in Euljiro by collecting these things and selling them to avant-garde artists at a high price? He was innovative, too, having installed a motor on the cart so that he'd be able to pull the cart more easily.

"I'm sorry, but would you be willing to take them? I'll give them to you at a really good price. Ask your ma about me, the Jangchung-dong Missus. She knows everything. Let me talk to her."

I felt bad for these people, too, but their things went outside as well. Those who did business in the area came to claim their things within a few weeks, but there were many people I couldn't reach. In order to let the owners know I'd had to pay to discard their things, I wrote out a receipt for each person.

For the entire month, I cleaned the first and second floors. I then moved everything on the second floor to the first floor. Nothing else remained on the second floor except for the office. I mopped the floor every day until it sparkled. The young delivery guy from the Chinese restaurant said you could even skate on it. Happily, he dashed around the warehouse in his sneakers.

I gave Kim Yeongchul a call. I wanted to ask her what I should do about the empty second floor. Roaming about somewhere in the mountains, she didn't pick up. Even her friends said it'd been a while since they last saw her. Regardless, the rent for the building was withdrawn each month from the bank account she signed over to me. There was no money coming in, but I still had to pay the utility bills and miscellaneous expenses, so it looked like I would have to close down the business when I'd just inherited it. But I wasn't going to let her come home and rip up our contract because of my incompetence. I wouldn't let her hurt my pride that way.

The flyer I'd distributed around the market had been pointless. Some said it was too long, so they didn't want to read it, and others said they had nothing they needed to put in storage.

For three months, nothing happened and nothing helped the business. I even went to saunas, internet cafes, churches, playgrounds, old buildings along the Cheonggye Stream to hand out flyers. Just looking at them made me feel sick. But when I found myself standing before the empty warehouse, I felt motivated to try once more.

I went inside Sindang Creative Mall one night. While walking around, I suddenly recalled seeing a sign for shrimp fried rice at one of the restaurants and thought eating it would satiate my hunger. There were only a few shrimps in the fried rice, but the strong shrimp smell was enough to calm my nerves.

The underground mall sought by only a few people had a very low ceiling and was as quiet as inside the belly of a fish. When I stood outside a store selling uniforms, I couldn't help but smile. I looked at every kind of uniform there was and then peered into the studios that lined the arcade. I walked slowly past the studios, careful not to distract the artists who sat with their backs turned, staring into laptop screens or glaring at documents, as if meditating or dreaming. I stood before a studio where a poster with a geometric design was stuck on the window and snapped a picture with my cell phone. A woman, who'd just finished making a dainty pair of earrings, smiled at me as she put them on the shelf above the display. For a moment, her bloodshot eyes lingered in my mind.

Then one night, it happened. The power went out at the mall. It might have been for a very short time. I couldn't see anything. I heard snickering. I walked down the dark hall, my hands stretched out before me, as if I'd become a spirit that roams the arcade at night. With each step, I could see a little further ahead. A radioactive contamination meter dangled around my neck, like some toy. The darkness brightened into a brown and I saw the path that led to Pripyat. The bumpy mud road, the children of Pripyat wearing radioactive contamination meters around their necks, who looked at me with hollow eyes. Up ahead burly men pointed their radiation detection wands toward the sky and pressed a button. A forest of naked gray trees grew thick, and I heard a loud rustle and the earth shook. My feet sank into the ground up to my ankles and the children called my name. Wolves glared at me from a distance, their eyes glittering. The children shouted.

Do you hear the siren? Do you hear it ringing? Stay away from here.

One by one, flashlights turned on. A light shook. When the power came back on, I had my face pressed against the window of a hanbok dress shop. The gaudy colors that filled towel shops and yarn shops became superimposed on Pripyat's streets. My palms were damp with sweat.

• • •

On April 26 of 1986, I lived in the city of Pripyat near Chernobyl in what was previously known as the Soviet Union. Due to the accident at the nuclear power plant, we were forced to evacuate. I was somehow carried on the wind and ended up coming all the way here to Hwanghak-dong. Pripyat has now become a ghost town, but many elderly people have gone back. Though they were diagnosed with cancer, they went back, saying they wanted to die there. I run a storage business that's named after Pripyat. I am fated to die from cancer. I already know. Those who believe you'll die from cancer one day, those who'll have to store the things that your dead friend leaves behind, those heading somewhere with no hope of return—why don't you bring them all to Pri Storage?

I'd made another flyer one day when the noise of the excavator had seemed unusually loud. It was much shorter than the last one. I really liked it. It was perhaps the last thing I could do.

I folded the flyers in half. After pressing them down with my palm and putting them in my bag, I went to the underground mall. I was convinced that the only ones who could save me were the artists sitting in their cramped studios, making something with their hands. I pushed flyers through the crack in the door and handed some directly to artists who were still working, not having gone home yet. I didn't care whether they used the flyers as trivets to put under scalding tteokbokki or if they went in the trash.

When I'd finished distributing all the flyers, Hwanghak-dong was dark, covered in yellow dust. I crossed the street and went past the playground and saw the orange lamps next to the women's sewing machines. The women didn't bother to spread open the flyers I handed them. They simply kept pushing fabric through the machines.

A few days later, my first customer came. I jumped up from my chair and bowed respectfully, folding my body in half.

"Welcome, can I help you?"

It was a woman wearing a long mink coat over a blue pajama set. Her body seemed very thin compared to her large head. Reeking of perfume, cigarette smoke, and an odd odor, she looked like a difficult woman. She raked her fingers through her long wavy hair and blinked her large black eyes.

"Can I keep my luggage here? For about three months?"

I went down to the first floor and dragged the two suitcases sitting at the bottom of the stairs up to the second floor. They were plastered with airport baggage claim stickers from unfamiliar places. The woman kept fiddling with her phone while she filled out the form, entered her contact information, and paid the deposit. When I handed her the deposit slip, she wrote down her address, and in the contents box, the word *clothes* in English. She then rubbed her forehead a few times, as if she had a lot to think about.

"Would you like some coffee?"

The customer who came in the next day was also a woman. She looked prim in a black belted coat with shoulder-length hair. She brought me downstairs and opened the trunk of her car that was parked behind the warehouse by the construction site fence. We carried many bags back up to the office where she filled out the form, sitting with her back straight and legs pressed together.

"I got a divorce, but I have some things that are a bit difficult to deal with. I'd like to keep them here."

"Can I get you a cup of coffee?"

2007, 2008, 2009 . . . The years lapped like waves and drifted away. I was a bit older, but I wasn't yet diagnosed with thyroid cancer. Sometimes I had a dream about walking into Pripyat, my home. Under stormy clouds, I passed the forest where wild animals lived and saw the city limit sign for Pripyat. A dark, heavy wind blew on the path leading into the city. The old men and women who'd once left the city to avoid radiation exposure now waited for their deaths, eating stale bread. They opened their windows and gestured toward me to come closer. No matter how much I walked, the sky was overcast and stormy clouds descended on my head. I was short of breath, but strangely enough, I felt at peace.

"Why do you keep going to the mountains?" I asked my mother. Kim Yeongchul, the first generation of Best Storage, was climbing the mountains around the country. One day, I realized she looked better, healthier than me. She'd come to the market to buy a new hiking outfit, because the one she'd first bought was worn out.

"Then do you expect me to start going to church at this age? Or to mass? If you were me, where would you go?"

She was a strange woman. I simply couldn't understand her second phase of life. After drinking a cup of Maxim instant coffee, she got up and headed for the mountains again.

Business was so good there wasn't enough storage space. Maybe I'd become successful after all. The negative side to this kind of work was that it was easy to get a sense of someone else's life. Other than that, everything was fine. Without fail all the tenants paid their monthly fees and followed the rules. The only thing they didn't abide by was something I mentioned in the very beginning. That they should never light any candles in the warehouse. But they lit them as soon as walked in, as if out of habit.

One tenant, after losing her boyfriend in an accident, started going on trips. As soon as she saved up enough money from working, she took off. She brought her boyfriend's desk and moved it to a corner on the second floor of the warehouse. She placed his journal, notebooks, color pens, and the books he'd liked on his desk, just as he'd left them. His cell phone was always charging, placed in the cradle. She sometimes played the music he'd liked. All I had to do was give her a cup of coffee and set up a portable heater for her so that she wouldn't feel cold. She would dial a number on her phone and the phone on the cradle would start to vibrate. She'd then listen to his ringtone with her eyes closed.

There was another tenant. He was a musician who'd been studying the guitar. Back when he'd lived in the States, he'd dreamed of combining Korean music and western music to develop a new style of guitar music. Though it had been a difficult time, he'd been happy. Then one winter day as he was getting off the bus, the tips of the fingers on his right hand tingled. He'd been walking toward SoHo in the dazzling sun, but a strange premonition compelled him to step into an alley. He stopped and gazed down at his numb fingers.

He brought the guitar and sheet music from when he'd studied music to the warehouse. Though he couldn't play anymore, he couldn't get rid of his guitar. So at the warehouse, he tuned the guitar or polished the body until it shone. Sometimes when he turned his head to look out the window through which the afternoon light flooded in, I got chills. He looked more handsome than any musician in the world, so much so that I almost put my arms around him.

There was a customer who brought in books that had belonged to her daughter. The girl had died from illness before she was able to bloom. Though other family members gradually forgot, memories of the girl only grew more vivid for her as time passed. There was another customer who brought in the colorful imported china that had filled her kitchen cupboards when she'd been wealthy, as well as a heap of housedresses from her closet. And there was a distinguished government worker who asked if he could store a thick folder of articles about a famous female celebrity. He said it would be disrespectful to this actress if his wife were to find out and call him crazy and take his folder away. Under each article was the newspaper name, title of the article, and his brief impressions.

A tenant who was a photographer turned his unit into a darkroom. He was a friend of a metalsmith who had a studio in the mall. His photo enlarger looked like a piece of junk in the dark, but when he was there, it transformed into something different. Whenever he came, the whole warehouse seemed alive with energy, but more than anything, his cologne lingered in the air for a long time so that every time I opened the office door, I couldn't think straight.

I wasn't sure if the tendency to collect things was a regional or individual characteristic of Hwanghak-dong folks, but they entrusted me with things that were somewhat unusual, such as commemorative items, insignia, military uniforms, and scary objects like shotguns from the Vietnam War. Old men with wrinkled faces came to the warehouse and put on their military uniforms decorated with red badges. They sauntered around the warehouse, their shoes buffed to a shine.

And of course there is a Pripyat corner in this warehouse. A place for my souvenirs, a place I haven't shown anyone.

"Would you be able to accept a monkey?"

"I have an alligator I was raising at home. . ."

Surprisingly, many people have asked if they could keep their pets here. Though I can't accept them yet, I'm planning to accept them soon, as well as frightful animals, cremated remains with no resting place, stopped clocks. Death, memory, and the past. After all, it was Pripyat Storage's policy to store things you couldn't possibly find a place for anywhere else.

Processions

THE MOMENT THE MOVIE STOPPED, the woman was hunched over with her gaze fixed on the screen, trying to unstick something from the heel of her shoe. The film had been approaching its climax when it stuttered and eventually stopped. "Jeez," she said, stamping her foot. It wasn't the first time it was being shown in Seoul, but there was no knowing when it would be screened again. Whenever a film exhibition was held, she'd watched each film, thinking she may never see it again. She couldn't help feeling flustered. No, what she was feeling was more complicated and disappointing. She didn't know what to do.

The theater lobby was very hot and dry. People drifted out into the lobby and waited for the film to resume. The woman gazed blankly at the doors through which people entered and exited. A gust of wind rushed in every time the doors opened and closed. She went to the bathroom and stood before the mirrors that lined multiple walls. She glanced down at her watch to check the time. Eight o'clock. The film had stopped after about an hour. It took some time to locate her makeup pouch from her oversized purse. Even though she tried to keep her purse organized, the inside was always a mess. At last, she fished out her pouch, put on some lip-gloss, and washed her hands. She looked in the mirror. People were still waiting in the lobby.

The one thing she had been doing consistently until now was watching movies at the Cinematheque. Instead of sponsoring a child in Southeast Asia or Africa by sending ten- to twenty-thousand won a month like some people or giving an offering at church, she paid a fee of one hundred thousand won per year to become a member of the Cinematheque, attending nearly all the events that were held in this old building. So even in the middle of summer after the rainy season, when many people were away on vacation, she came to the theater and watched a film with a small audience. For her, films were more than just films.

Just as people make certain preparations before going on a date with someone they want to impress, she also had a ritual before watching a film. In the previous week, she'd even gone to the mall, though she thought women who spent their entire day going from store to store on every floor were out of their minds. But that day, she had stood before the directory, glancing at the location of every shop from the lowest floor to the top floor. Though she hated going to crowded places, being alone in the middle of a crowd was tolerable.

Still it took less than ten minutes to pick a comfortable blouse and try it on before buying it. Because she didn't like paper shopping bags, she asked for a plastic bag instead, and then put the bag in her purse. After using the bathroom, she was waiting for the elevator when she was suddenly gripped by terror. She panicked because she couldn't see outside, because the building could very well crumple like a piece of paper. Unable to wait for the elevator any longer, she rushed past the shops and took the escalator down.

She thought of the one thing that could banish her terror: the marine park, built on land artificially reclaimed from the sea. It was her favorite of all the places she'd ever visited. She smiled, thinking of the time she had gone there. An abandoned dog with a skin disorder had been the lone visitor, shivering and roaming around the park. It disappeared soon after. She dragged a small log over to the sand, stretched out on it, and read a book. Spread behind her were the city buildings and the bridge that was arched like a bow, connecting the reclaimed land to the mainland. Waves danced before her. She didn't see even a common crow.

When she was there, she experienced for the first time a moment that was free from visions. The smashed face of a corpse, a trail of bloody footprints leading from the front gate to the door, sagging bruised skin, stuffed toys grinning widely with missing eyes, a broad-shouldered man who's dragging along an exploded suitcase, leaving behind a single shoe covered in blood. These awful visions that were like scenes from a horror movie had filled her head. But there at that park, they had no longer assaulted her.

For some reason, the woman had always been plagued by horrific illusions. At first, she googled *dream interpretation* and read up on the subject, also consulting books on psychoanalysis, but it was no use. The more she focused on her problem, the more these visions haunted her, until they gradually invaded her everyday life.

It was strange that she was fine only at the marine park. The temperature gradually rose and fat jellyfish washed up along the shore. She poked the translucent bodies with her fingers and prodded them with her toes.

In the distance, there was a man lying shirtless. He got up and stretched, swinging his arms. Neither of them strolled along the quiet coast. On their own, they enjoyed as much beach and sunlight as they were given. It was peaceful.

She took refuge in this landscape. Never would she infringe on someone else's time out of curiosity. She despised people like that. She believed that act was worse than stealing and murdering. That's why she was always alone after a certain age, but she wasn't lonely.

People still loitered in the lobby. Cell phones went off here and there and the coffee machine was running. She moved into the hallway and gazed at the poster of Werner Herzog's vampire movie on a column. She ran her palm over the long nails barely stuck to the ends of the vampire's fingers. Right then, a staff member came out from the projection room and stood in the center of the lobby.

"We're deeply sorry for the wait. We tried our best, but it'll be difficult to resume the screening tonight. We'll schedule a re-screening as soon as possible and notify you by email or text. Have a good night and we apologize again for the inconvenience."

She looked up at the ceiling, feeling as if the sky were falling. She was stunned. The lobby emptied soon after, but she continued to stand in the same spot. A single red glove that someone had left behind was draped over a table edge. She walked toward the table and stretched the glove this way and that, peering at it to see if any parts were worn out. Suddenly, she turned toward the theater. She stepped inside, hearing a sound come from the projection room. She walked toward the front where the light was shining dimly and took a seat.

She sensed people moving about in the projection room. The film was still playing. The film stuttered forward until it reached the scene where it had been cut short, and then stopped once more. That's when she saw him. The back of the head of a man who sat in the front row, waiting for the film to resume.

"I don't know when they'll show it again," he said, after they'd left the Cinematheque. She didn't know if he was talking to himself, so she simply kept walking. "What a bummer," he said.

She found him odd, but she had no choice but to walk with him to the elevator. When the elevator didn't come up, he started to hurry down the stairs. She was forced to use the stairs, too.

The back of his Land Rover was caked with dirt, and there were dusty gray streaks on his backpack, as if it had scraped against something. Just as she'd suspected, the elevator was stuck on the ground floor, with several men loading furniture onto it.

The man and woman crossed the street, leaving a bit of space between them.

"Alrighty then. See you," he said, bowing his head.

He clomped ahead until she called after him. "Excuse me!"

• • •

He'd come straight from a hike. Though he didn't particularly like movies, he liked to watch one as soon as he came down the mountain. He couldn't tell which of the two was his objective, but it was undeniable that watching movies had become a hobby. When he'd worked at an office, he'd been extremely envious of people who'd go watch a movie in the middle of the day. But now when he came across office workers in a theater, he felt worried for them.

He went hiking several times a week. He didn't know exactly when, but he'd started sometime in the spring, the year after he'd quit his job. He recalled the bleak wind that had thrust into his sleeves and hiking boots. Now whenever he went up a mountain, he no longer felt like a person. Instead he felt as if he'd become a part of the wind, the landscape, or the mountain itself.

At first, he'd been so out of breath and his legs so sore that he'd barely made it halfway up a 600-meter mountain. He'd kept stopping to drink water and eat chocolate. He didn't make eye contact with the older women who sat drinking coffee in twos and threes, starting conversations with the other hikers. He also ignored the loud cheers and chants of students from a university hiking club.

He didn't go to the mountains because he enjoyed it. In short, he was a failure. But the last thing he wanted to do was to go around telling people he had no idea how he'd become a failure, while sponging beer and wine off them and earning their pity. He started putting his life in order. He cleaned out his closet and tossed his CDs, even the books he'd cherished. He made a spreadsheet to calculate his net worth, but after subtracting his liabilities from his assets, the sum was zero. He gathered his certificates of insurance and put them in a plastic folder. He threw away greeting cards containing typical messages and platitudes, and put all the notes, certificates, and photos from elementary school and high school in a separate plastic folder and numbered them.

In the end, his remaining possessions fit in three cardboard boxes. He couldn't believe he'd worked so hard to lug these things around until now, things that would fit in just three boxes. On the one hand, he was agitated that there was nothing truly decent he could call his own. Yet, he still felt he possessed too many things. Memories from childhood, friends and peers, names of things he'd liked, performance reviews, manufacturer information, et cetera. His head was too full of clutter, just as when he'd worked at an office. He was relieved he didn't have a wife or children.

In his wallet, he always carried his resident registration card with his current address, driver's license, and an old business card, so that he could be easily identified if something were to happen. He wished that day would come quickly, so that everything would be over. He wrote nothing, neither emails nor journal entries. He got rid of his cell phone as well and made no calls.

On some days, his mouth reeked of something awful, and on other days one side of his head hurt so much he thought his ear would start bleeding. If he was having an extremely hard time, he turned on music and sobbed out loud or did a handstand. But still, if the pain was unbearable, he drank multiple bottles of soju and slept like a corpse. Then he'd be sapped of all strength and have no energy to cry, even if he wanted to. He believed the liquor had dried up his whole body.

On the days he wanted to talk, he rambled to himself all day long. You think that makes sense? I've got a lot to say, too. Have you hiked up a mountain before? What did I do wrong? I'm sorry, but that won't work. You think you know how it feels to be crazy like me?

A few months before, he had decided to rent out his house located outside Seoul. The realtor said it would probably take some time to find tenants, since the house was old and the neighborhood was far from desirable. However, it had been rented out right away. He'd easily accepted the tenant's request to move in first, even though their deposit wasn't quite ready.

The day he was supposed to collect the rest of the payment, he pushed open the front gate of the shabby traditional house with the tile roof he'd lived in until recently. The tenants could have simply wired him the money, but he didn't know when he'd be able to see his old home again, so he'd insisted on coming himself to collect the payment. His heart throbbed from the late summer heat and the savory smell of cooking. Whenever he'd stepped through the doors of one of these old traditional houses facing the highway, he'd felt as if he were on his way to die. He'd simply waited for morning to come so that he could leave the house.

But it was different that day. He doubted what he was seeing—the bright lights shining out from the windows, the laughter, vigor, and warmth. He couldn't believe it was the same dark, gloomy house he'd lived in. Feeling miserable, he stood outside the door, unable to go in.

A woman in a white sweater with her hair tied in a ponytail came out carrying a pot and noticed him.

"Oh, you're already here!" she cried, greeting him as if he were a relative. She'd recognized him right away, despite having seen him only once at the realtor's office.

"Oh, come in! Why don't you join us for dinner?"

As though she really knew him, she grasped him by the arm and dragged him into the dark room he'd lived in until a few weeks before.

The room, which had been like a cave, now sported pink floral wallpaper, and felt like the chamber of a princess, as if it were floating in air. The woman's husband jumped to his feet to shake his hand, and he found himself seated before the low table. Joining them was still another—a toddler squirming in a walker, stuffing the rice ball in his hand into his mouth.

The dinner was humble, simply some kimchi, tofu stew, and roasted seaweed you dipped in soy sauce, but he had never enjoyed such a delicious meal, even though he'd eaten at plenty of fancy restaurants specializing in Spanish, French, and all sorts of fusion fare, served by polite waitstaff.

These people gave off a different air, too. Like the baby, the woman's cheeks were pink and her skin taut. He thought she looked like a red lily, plump and well-watered. He'd never met someone with such a friendly voice and such color in her cheeks. Even her husband looked young and healthy, uncorrupted by life.

After receiving an envelope containing the rest of the deposit on which the words "Thank you" were written in tiny print, he stepped out of the house but continued to linger outside the gate. He climbed up onto the entrance stoop and peered into the bright courtyard for some time before he finally left.

The next day when he hiked up the mountain, he couldn't help thinking that everything looked different. He wanted to ask: Did mountains have no thoughts? Is that why they stood in the same place day after day? For a long time, he gazed at the tree trunks firmly rooted in the earth, but they remained the same.

• • •

The woman had trouble waking in the morning. She could hardly lift her head or her legs. Much later, she learned her low blood pressure was the cause. She lived simply, dividing her day into three parts and doing only a few things. She lacked the energy to carry out many activities. She didn't eat much, and she didn't exercise at all. It had been a long time since she last talked to her friends.

If she went to the theater to watch a movie, she became so exhausted that she had to rest the next day. If she started a book, she couldn't do any other work until she finished it. It was very difficult for her to go to the hair salon and explain how she wanted her hair cut, so she went to a beauty supply store and bought scissors. She couldn't imagine going to the market to bargain and haggle over the price, so she usually ordered her groceries online.

But these everyday things weren't the problem. She was haunted by awful visions. Even if it was raining and snowing, and the scenery outside was lovely and romantic, nightmares unfolded as soon as she closed her eyes. Strange visions that had come out of nowhere. In them, she stabbed someone to death or she stood on a riverbank in an unfamiliar city, looking down at a corpse crawling with maggots. Or she couldn't run away, because her legs were tied up, and after repeated attempts to flee when she would finally wake, she'd rub her lips and blood would come off on her hands. She'd look in the mirror to find her lip had cracked from the dry indoor air.

What she found most difficult was being with people. She saw some friends she hadn't seen in a while. As soon as they sat down, though no one had asked, they began to talk about their children, and then their husbands, and even their husbands' families, finally asking her why she hadn't yet married. She became so angry she vowed never to see these shallow bores who had nothing better to talk about. She thought it would be better to cut ties with them for good.

She grew even more enraged when one of the friends called the next day. "We were worried. We thought maybe you felt left out, since you're not married."

Her whole body started shaking, and unable to take it anymore, she ended up shouting. "You all seem to love being married, but I don't want to associate with a bunch of shallow morons who have nothing to talk about except marriage and families. Don't ever call me again." With that, she hung up. Enraged that she'd revealed her true feelings, she paced back and forth in her apartment, pounding her chest with her fist.

During the week she went to the library, and on the weekends she went to a concert in the park held by environmental groups. She was able to relax a little, watching children sing and play with the punching ball. If she wandered through the flea market, cute boutiques, and the large Kyobo Bookstore, the week flew by. If only she didn't have those nightmares, if only she didn't see those gruesome images, there was nothing more she wanted from her simple life.

• • •

The woman and man headed to a Coffee Bean. They each ordered and paid for their own drink. Unlike the woman, the man took a while to order. She glanced at him from the table. *He sure is particular about his coffee.* She thought he was extremely plain looking. There was nothing striking about his appearance at all.

"What do you call a sad cup of coffee?" he asked once he'd finished ordering and come to the table.

"I'm not sure. I don't know things like that."

"A depresso," he said, raising his finger.

She was so stunned she didn't even laugh. But she couldn't help snickering a moment later.

He had ordered a strong cup of espresso. He said something about coffee, but she couldn't understand for the life of her.

"Where do you get that kind of information?" she asked.

"Oh, around," he said. "The film was just getting interesting when it stopped. Whenever something like that happens, I always wonder if I'll get to watch it again," he said, raising the espresso cup that was just big enough to cover his lips.

She tried to make an expression, which would convey that what he'd said was both sensible and wistful. However, she was so shocked that this man sitting across from her had shared the same thought as her. Neither of them had much to say. Gradually, she turned her attention elsewhere until they were both watching the people who walked past the café with coffees in hand and collars buttoned to the top.

Right then, the woman felt an unbearable itchiness, as if insects were crawling all over her. *What if this man drags me off somewhere?* Suddenly she was seized with fear and she pushed her chair back a little from the table. From that moment on, everything about the man—his clothes, his hairstyle, his shoes—seemed strange. Even the fact that he was wearing hiking clothes on a weekday seemed strange. She chewed her lips, wanting to settle this situation as quickly as possible. She opened her mouth soon after, as if she'd just remembered something.

"I traveled outside Korea only once. My cousin was getting married to a Japanese man, so I went. The wedding was a bit strange. It would be quiet and then it would suddenly get noisy. After the wedding, I walked around downtown Tokyo for two days. I didn't know much about Tokyo, but I did want to visit the famous National Film Archive of Japan. The lobby there was packed with elderly people clasping small handbags on their knees. It was terribly quiet. Like they were all participating in a serious ceremony. Twenty minutes before the film started, the staff made us line up. I think the admission fee was 500 yen. Those who had trouble walking took the elevator and those who could walk used the stairs. They all acted as if they were participating in some kind of ritual, finding their seats without talking. The film began exactly on time. I think it was an Imamura Shōhei film. No other names are coming to mind, so that's probably right. The whole movie showed the everyday of a family, and then at the end, a nuclear bomb went off. I heard people weeping. The old women were crying. That's what the movie was about. After it was over, everyone walked down the stairs quietly, and some headed to the subway station and some disappeared around the corner. It was a weekday, and it didn't rain. I thought: I wish my city would have a theater like that, even when I'm old. Then I'd go every day. I remember thinking that."

Pointing at the Cinematheque they had come from, she added, "That there is that kind of place for me. I have to go now."

She jumped to her feet and left the coffeeshop. She walked as quickly as she could, scared he would follow her and grab her by the neck. She didn't look back. She walked past people and started to run.

She ran all the way to the bus stop and boarded a bus that had just arrived. After heading to an empty seat near the back, she looked straight ahead without turning around, as if the man were close behind. She felt as if the man would chase after her if she looked back. Her mouth ached from having talked too much.

• • •

The man was sitting at one of the low tables in the corner of the funeral home. An old colleague he'd been close to had called, saying his mother had passed away. When he'd worked at an office, he'd gone to countless funerals, but now the news of someone dying was both as unfamiliar as a message from outer space and as familiar as air.

"You look great. But look at us. Drinking's totally messed us up."

His old co-workers each had something to say. In the reception area, he ate peanuts while listening to them, but all the while, his gaze kept being pulled toward the doors through which people went in and out.

About an hour later, the person he'd been waiting for finally made an appearance. Misuk. He couldn't help but speak her name aloud. She went to offer her condolences, dressed in a black suit and white dress shirt with her hair in a ponytail. After stepping out of the mortuary, she scanned the low tables. He ended up dropping the peanut he was holding, wondering whether she was going to come this way or leave because of another engagement. "Chief Kim, over here!" someone cried. Smiling, she moved toward where he was sitting.

He waited for her to acknowledge him, after she'd finished nodding at the others. It had been a very long time.

"Wow, how long has it been?" she finally said to him. He could neither laugh nor cry and simply nodded at her. He put his hand over the dish and grabbed a fistful of peanuts.

She had aged quite a bit. He noticed the marionette lines that had started to form around her mouth, and the hair on the crown of her head seemed a bit sparse, but more than anything, she looked somewhat frumpy. He laughed to himself, thinking about the time they had spent together. The voices of the other guests faded from his mind until all he could hear were her deep chuckles. Wrapping his arms around his knees, he looked down and laughed. It was because he had suddenly recalled her unique laughter.

People kept trickling in. He got up from his seat, feeling both awkward and bored. He gazed down at the sea of black dress shoes filling the entrance and a wave of vertigo hit him. An overweight young man he assumed was part of the bereaved family was straightening the shoes with a pair of tongs. The man took the escalator down. The air outside was very cold. People gathered around the ashtray, smoking or gazing vacantly up at the sky. He didn't know whether he should simply leave, now that he was outside, or go back in and talk to his old colleagues.

"It's awkward, isn't it?"

He was shocked to find Chief Kim standing next to him.

She fished out a pack of cigarettes from her purse and stuck one in her mouth. "You want one?"

He shook his head and smiled. She felt masculine to him all of a sudden. "I see you still haven't kicked the habit."

"You're doing good?" she said, blowing out smoke. "Let's have lunch sometime."

"Sure." He couldn't help feeling that she'd let herself go. Her sloppy speech and her edginess, as if she'd become bitter.

"You sure nothing's going on?" he asked.

She looked up at the sky. "Of course not. What could possibly be going on with boring office workers like us?"

The man laced his fingers together. He felt awkward, but he didn't know what to say that would dispel the awkwardness.

"I'm gonna go. Can you tell Manager Chung and the director that I had to take off?"

She extinguished her cigarette in the ashtray and crossed her arms over her chest. "All right. Goodbye," she said with a slight bow.

"Go back in. It's really cold."

Just as he was climbing into a cab, she turned and called out in a loud voice, "Did you know I went to your place to see you? Just once!"

The man sat in the passenger seat and gazed at the raindrops falling on the windshield. Her voice still lingered in his ears. He felt an odd sensation, as if something like a rock had been dislodged from his chest. Even the wide turns the cab was making unsettled him that he was afraid to look out the window. Misuk, he muttered again. For the rest of the ride home, he kept his gaze down. He didn't look up once.

• • •

A poster advertising the Friends of the Cinematheque festival hung outside the building. Once again, people gathered outside the ticket booth. Throughout the entire film, the woman kept scanning the audience to see if she recognized a certain head shape. Even if he wasn't there, she hoped the film would not stop again.

The screening went smoothly. As always, most films didn't live up to their reputation. Before the start of a film, a few days before the screening—these times were always more exciting. What is it about movies that captivates people? she often wondered. But she thought about the opposite case more often. Why do I cling to movies this way? What if they betray me one day? What if the theater disappears, where would I go then? What would happen if no one made movies anymore?

"Oh, you're here again," he said to the woman, who was making her way to the elevator.

She was so surprised she jerked to a stop. "You scared me!" she said, covering her mouth with her hand.

He was dressed in the same black hiking clothes from last time. "How about a coffee somewhere?" he asked her nonchalantly.

Though she thought he was odd, she found herself following him. She was relieved she didn't feel scared or guarded like last time.

They went to a Starbucks across from the subway station. Once again, the man took a long time to order. She noticed the dirt on the crotch of his pants.

"What do you call a wise cup of coffee?" he asked her once he'd finished ordering and come to the table.

"I'm not sure. I don't know things like that." She replied the same way she had before.

He raised his finger again and said, "Bean there, done that."

Stunned once more, she didn't even laugh. But this time again, she couldn't help snickering a moment later.

Right then, she recalled a scene from a movie she'd once seen. A man and woman meet for the first time and start speaking to each other, trading witty, movie-worthy lines. *We're strangers meeting for the first time. What's something only strangers can do together? We'll do only those things. After this, let's promise to never meet again. We'll just talk about things that strangers can tell each other, okay? Shall we walk all night? Or should we go to a hotel? We met each other for the first time today.*

It was a strange movie. She couldn't remember what the two people finally did, how they'd spent their time, or what they'd felt in the end. All she could recall is that they had talked endlessly. They had sat in a café where a stream of people came and went, talking endlessly and sharing thoughts to one another.

More and more, the man found himself looking into this woman's eyes. She was neither attractive nor pretty, but her face had an odd innocence about it. He couldn't gauge her age, her line of work, or even her personality, which were usually easy enough to guess. In fact, the man rarely met strangers, let alone carried on a conversation with one.

They talked haltingly until the Starbucks closed at eleven o'clock. Because there was no reason to see each other again, they spoke more freely. They talked about the times they had been most hurt, times that they had been most angry, without going through the trouble of providing context. They were free to exaggerate and package the story however they wanted. In the end, they decided to each pick an activity they could do together as strangers.

A few days later, she waited for him at the train station. Because of her nightmares from the previous night, she was almost late. He was wearing a windbreaker over the hiking clothes he always wore. Perhaps neither of them had slept well, because as soon as they boarded the train and sat down, they fell asleep, hardly noticing their heads were touching.

They arrived at the destination past three o'clock in the afternoon. He couldn't help thinking it was strange place that was neither inland nor an island. Trees with long narrow leaves were planted in groups of two or three in the middle of the road where the bus passed. They went into a teahouse with an old woodstove, drank tea, and looked out the tinted windows at the unfamiliar city. There weren't many people, cars, or houses. There were more signs and billboards, and they also saw many houses that stood empty.

She made a phone call. She kept glancing at his face, as though no one was picking up on the other end of the line.

"Actually, I was born here," she said. Unable to get through, she was starting to grow frustrated. "A distant relative wanted to see me. And there's a place we need to visit today."

The man nodded.

After making their way out of the teahouse, they boarded a bus, crossed the river, and got off in front of the Forest Service. She wandered around the low-rise, finally knocking on the door of a small shop with a sign that said Real Estate. She kept knocking, but no one came to the door.

She called again. No one answered. She knocked on the office door once more. After a long time, an old man opened the door with a bang.

"Who're you?"

The second he opened his mouth, the putrid stench of liquor swept over them.

"It's me. You told me to come," she said.

"Let me get dressed first. But you sure don't look like your ma at all."

The only place to sit inside was at the end of a small sofa. The cluttered office looked as if it would collapse any second.

"And who's that you got there? Your husband?" the old man yelled from the inside room, sticking his face out to show his toothless mouth.

"He's a paralegal I brought along."

The man didn't feel good about her cold voice, or the fact that she'd lied about him being a solicitor. But a paralegal was better than a boyfriend or husband.

The old man started the beat-up car parked beside the office. The man and woman crawled awkwardly into the backseat. The car reeked of liquor.

"You realize you're drinking and driving, don't you?" she snapped.

They sped along the narrow road until they finally pulled into a driveway to the only crematorium in the city. Once they'd been traveling over the bumpy lane for some time, she saw a kind of fog before them.

"Do you see that mountain ridge up ahead? That's your grandfather's legacy."

However, the woman heaved a loud sigh before he could finish his sentence.

The car stopped on top of a hill that afforded a good view of the ridge. It was hardly a mountain, the sides having been gouged out and some places shaved down. The trees had all been cut down and a thick black mesh covered some of the slopes.

"That right there is her grandfather's legacy. Look, this is the proof. If she can get it back, she'll be rich. Do you know what I had to do to get to this point? No one ever treated me to a meal or a drink, but I did my best. All I'm asking for is the commission."

The old man pulled out some rolled-up documents from the center console and shook them before the man's eyes.

"Just gimme ten or twenty million won for the initial cost," he said, sticking a cigarette in his mouth. "That's all I ask. It's a win-win situation,"

"I don't have any money. But if you manage to get the land and you're able to sell it for me, I'll give you the money then."

The old man stubbed out his cigarette, annoyed. "God, she's impossible to talk to. Her ma was the same way. Their whole family was."

The man turned and looked up toward the top of the crematorium. The woman's face couldn't look any colder, and the land that was supposedly worth several billion won looked like a ruin.

"I came today because you told me to come, but please don't call me anymore. I don't care about this mountain.

What could it be worth? If you can, you sell it and keep the profit. Just don't bother me anymore."

The old man frowned. "Jeez, you're impossible. That's no way to be."

They drove to the city in his old car. At his insistence that he needed some soup to cure his hangover, they went into a restaurant. While he drank some more, he repeated what he'd said over and over again. The woman stood up and stuffed an envelope inside his pocket. After they stepped out of the restaurant, the old man climbed back in his car and drove off under the influence. She gazed after the car in silence for some time.

• • •

"Do you know when the boat will leave?" the woman asked a server at the teahouse.

"Which boat do you mean?"

"For the funeral today . . ."

Around sunset, the woman and man watched the seaside funeral, which was a custom of the region. They listened to the faint murmur of the river as they waited for the procession to pass. They could only see a haze of empty space. Rowboats appeared and disappeared on the river like ghosts. She couldn't forget the funeral processions she'd seen as a child from this place. When a procession would pass by, she would let out a deep breath, perhaps because she couldn't help feeling anew that she was alive, or because the dead had been properly sent off.

A long procession moved slowly from the right side of the river, far from where they were standing, to the left. Small children trailed the procession. Even dogs followed, as well as bicycles.

It went on and on. She could guess where the body was laid. As the sun set, she could see a red torch burning at the end of the procession. She heard the ringing of a bell and something like a song or wailing. She thought maybe these sounds were the crying of animals that lived in the river.

The man stood back and watched the woman following the procession toward the shore. Her hands were clasped together in front of her, and she stepped forward like a child who had done something wrong. Though there wasn't anyone directing them, the people in white mourning clothes seemed to know where they were supposed to go.

It was hard to tell which was the water and which was the sky. The torches burned, and the procession that looked as if it would continue all night turned toward the river and came to a stop. They brought their torches together and everyone stood watching a particular spot for a long time. The torches burned higher. The sound of the bell grew louder, and even the sound of the river grew louder. A wail broke out. Right then, the man saw the stunted silhouette of the woman who stood motionless, as if she'd committed a grave wrong. Everything grew dark. How much time had passed? A long white plume of smoke unfurled.

• • •

A few days later, they met again at the Cinematheque. Fortunately, the film screening went off without a hitch. There were many people, perhaps because winter was coming to an end. The two met in the lobby after the screening and exchanged bows at the same time.

It was the man's turn to pick the activity. What he wanted was to go to a certain ramen shop located on a busy street.

"That's it?" the woman said.

The man nodded.

The ramen broth was rich, hot, and greasy. She cocked her head, watching the man sweat while he ate, and thought that the world was full of odd people. Even his choice of activity—to go to a ramen shop—seemed odd. But she realized that she, too, was sweating.

Slowly, they walked down the crowded street. Their ears rang from the traffic and music.

"I'm sorry, but could you please wear something else besides that hiking outfit next time?" she asked.

He opened his eyes wide and laughed. "If you're gonna go there, I've got a lot to say about you, too."

"Then say it. What is it?" she asked, staring him in the face, but he said nothing.

KANG YOUNG-SOOK is the author of four novels, including the award-winning *Rina*, and five short story collections. Her work has appeared in *Granta*, *The White Review*, and other publications. She often writes about the female grotesque, delving into various genres, such as urban noir, fantasy, and climate fiction. Since her debut in 1998, she has received the Hanguk Ilbo Literature Prize, Kim Yujeong Literary Award, and Lee Hyo-seok Literature Award, among others.

JANET HONG is a writer and translator based in Vancouver, Canada. She received the TA First Translation Prize and the 16th LTI Korea Translation Award for her translation of Han Yujoo's *The Impossible Fairy Tale*. She's also a two-time winner of the Harvey Award for Best International Book for her translations of Keum Suk Gendry-Kim's *Grass* and Yeongshin Ma's *Moms*. Recent translations include Ha Seong-nan's *Bluebeard's First Wife* and Kwon Yeo-sun's *Lemon*.

Transit Books is a nonprofit publisher of international and American literature, based in Oakland, California. Founded in 2015, Transit Books is committed to the discovery and promotion of enduring works that carry readers across borders and communities. Visit us online to learn more about our forthcoming titles, events, and opportunities to support our mission.

TRANSITBOOKS.ORG